The Independent Bookworm

ABOUT THE BOOK

In 2002 ADR, the Empire of Argens is still reeling from the usurpation of its centuries-old throne by a ferocious dwarven warrior named Yula and his sorcerous human allies. Not only did they defeat the flower of elvish knighthood, but they exposed the former dynasty as demons in disguise.

Now a young captain, ruined by his loyalty to the old regime, has one last chance to redeem his family name in the officer training corps that's being established by the hated new emperor. Newly-graduated, Justin is convinced he has no future, and hearing the details of the secret mission he's assigned won't change his mind.

Civil War threatens the North Mark. Justin must race against time to form a company, and lead his men into the center of the web; but what happens when his loyalty to the Empire means the death of those who follow him?

"The Ring and the Flag" is the first story in the Shards of Light saga set in the Lands of Hope.

ABOUT THE AUTHOR

Will Hahn has been in love with heroic tales since age four, when his father read him the Lays of Ancient Rome and the Tales of King Arthur. He taught Ancient-Medieval History for years, but the line between this world and others has always been thin. The far reaches of fantasy, like the distant past, still bring him face to face with people like us, who have choices to make.

Will has written about the Lands of Hope since his college days (which by now are also part of ancient history). He chronicled the adventures of Solmn Judgement dilligently in two tomes of over 1000 pages each (it's now being published as an eBook series and in print) and his Shards of Light series, a sword and sorcery story. He also chronicled stand alone stories like "The Plane of Dreams" or "Three Minutes to Midnight." More of Will's tales of Hope are available at several online retailers.

Find out more on his website: www.WilliamLHahn.com

THE RING AND THE FLAG

Shards of Light
Volume I

William L. Hahn

The Ring and the Flag, Shards of Light I
– second edition –
published by the Independent Bookworm, USA und D
this book is also available as eBook at various retailers

printed On-Demand Publishing LLC, 100 Enterprise Way, Suite A200,
Scotts Valley, CA 95066, USA, www.createspace.com

ISBN-13 978-3-95681-094-7

Find more information on the publisher's website:
http://www.IndependentBookworm.de

For David Miller, shield-brother and fellow writer,
whose heroic career brings Hope to all in his company.

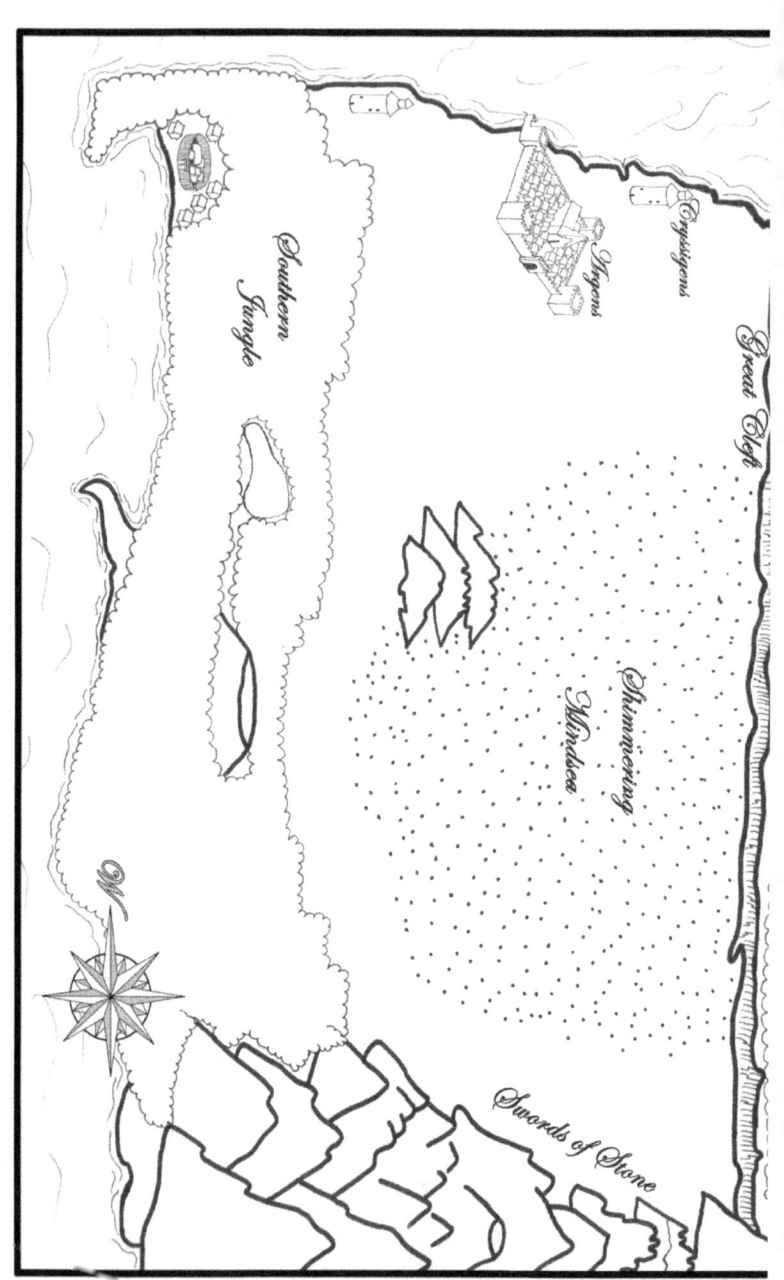

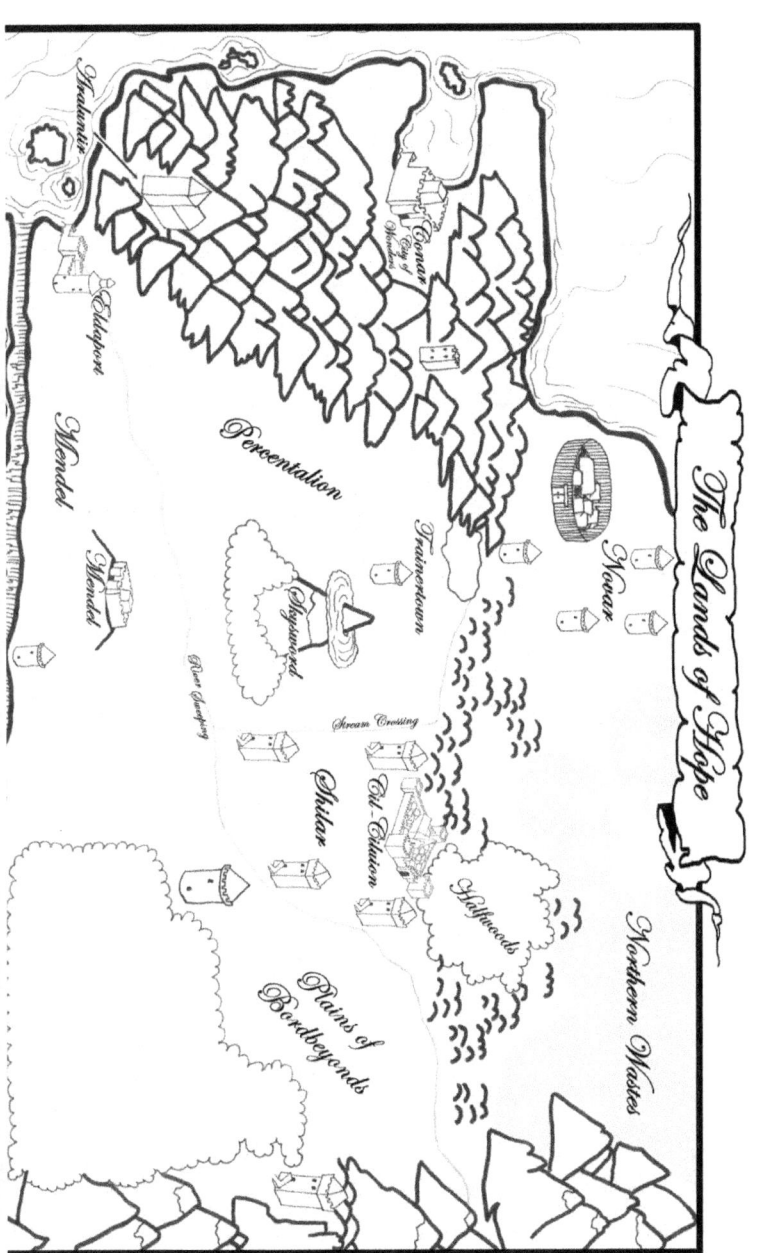

The Lands of Hope

Cast of Characters in Order of Appearance

Captain Justin Thyme	elf, graduate of Imperial officer training school in Argens
Commander of the Imperial Array Hansen	human, Leader of Emperor Yula's army
Dekentar Kein Trador	elf, "Strategos", noble-son enrolled in the Imperial Army
Emperor Yula	dwarf, also called the First or Usurper, Member of the Candidates, now ruler of the Argensian Empire
Captain Valin Th'lendor	elf, noble-son, Captain in the Imperial Army, rival of Justin
Dekentar M'nesa Zetee	elf, noble-son enrolled in the Imperial Army
Emperor Viridian XXVII	demon, Former emperor of Argens, demon in disguise, now slain
D'stagnon Kreel	elf, former Overlord of the North Mark, slain by Yula in 2001 ADR
Kreelon Kreel	elf, former Overlord of the North Mark, Son of Kreel, died after only months
Stealthic Morinack	Halfling, Emperor's Hand, Chief Intelligence Agent, former Candidate
Dekentar Tass	human, former gladiator enrolled in the Imperial Army
Far Mark Kallisthenes	elf, former gladiator now raised to rule of the Far Mark by Yula
Sirocco	war-stallion ridden by Valin
Furta	warhorse mare ridden by Justin
Skeer , Two-Eye	elf, bandit chief, Under orders to stop Argens' representative from reaching Cryssigens
Noudhal	elf, innkeeper of The Grog's Lees
Jonn Simith	elf, stone merchant just moved to Cryssigens
Minstrel Tambouri Shai	elf, Beautiful singer in Cryssigens
Giurid	elf, Brick-hauler, Blue House man
Smith Delith	elf, Female smith and tavern regular
Stealthic Feldspar	elf, disguised professional known across Cryssigens but never seen
Stealthic Trekelny	human, Greatest Stealthic of living memory, robbed Khoirah's temple and escaped the City of Heroes (*see Three Minutes to Midnight*)

THE RING AND THE FLAG

The Empire of Argens 2002 ADR

Justin's boots rang off the solid wood floor, bringing him pleasing echoes as they always did, even on this day, his last to dream of being an Imperial officer. Everything about the newly-built training quarters, from the square corners, spartan décor, and the smart, unpretentious attitude of accomplishment displayed by all his fellows—all of it had given him life for the past three months. Immersed in training, in the honest competition among other noble sons—the constant challenge to be his best, forget his heritage—Justin had thrived. Or thought he had. It was improper for an elf to show such emotion, but this was truly the final blow of misfortune. To have tried so hard, and done so well—he KNEW he had—only to wash out now, meant the end of the family line. From here, he couldn't imagine a future, any kind of future. He might catch on as a retainer to some minor knight in the farthest south. If he changed his name, or went east beyond the Shimmering Mindsea to join the former slaves and other castoffs re-colonizing the Far Mark, perhaps …

But the clean lines of the stockade and barracks brought him back, despite his gloom, to a sense of purpose. He was headed deep within the command center to his exit interview with Commander

Hansen. His steps took him to the junior officer's quarters, where over a dozen soldiers he knew spilled out of the sub-commander's office bearing the double-bars of a dekentar. Justin paused to salute every new officer he passed; though he had trained for the captain's sun-badge, from the moment these men donned those bars they outranked any cadet.

The return-salutes he received, and the words of greeting that accompanied them, were immediate but not enthusiastic. Justin saw men he had commanded in training, come to know a little and take the measure of. All of them worked well together with few exceptions—this new approach to the command of men, to craft a real profession of soldiering, had been a brilliant success and all of them could sense it. The wars he had known before, even the recent rebellion, were exposed now in Justin's memory as a formless clash of lances and swords by comparison.

The men of this corps, trained by the new emperor's right-hand man, had learned to seek advantage, to minimize obstacles, to force the terms of battle. Justin's name fell far in the war of the rebellion, and many of the new dekentars showed him they remembered, though their respect was quite intact. Yet one soldier in particular stepped out of his way to greet Justin. He saluted first, though his rank did not require it.

"Captain Justin, you would doubtless not recall me."

"Dekentar Kein Trador, greetings and congratulations," Justin said with a firm armgrip. The clear-eyed young officer did not scruple to suppress a grin to have graduated, and seemed even more pleased to be remembered. "Do you have a command assignment yet?"

"We are to await the Captains, sir, who will select us within the day."

"All success to you and your captain," Justin said as he turned to head onward with a heavy heart, knowing he would not be the one. Yet behind him Trador offered a parting compliment.

"I hope you have wished yourself good luck, sir." Justin turned back then and exchanged a look with the young man, and for a moment his heart dared to hope that he was wrong. But the grade-parchment rested inside his jacket, and no matter how many times he read it, the mark had been the same.

Moving down the inner corridor, Justin passed more dekentars exchanging congratulations, boasts, jokes. Over by an enormous window with waiting benches, a strapping tall human was roaring and slapping backs hard enough to knock men down. Justin recalled him vaguely, a single name only, something very short. He was amazed the man had graduated, but the double-bars were on his shoulders. And the mortal looked not in the least surprised, instead laughing with a kind of menacing grin Justin remembered from exercises. During one night mission, it proved difficult to restrain the man from actually hurting his fellow cadets. But then, no unit in the corps had climbed the hill-course more quickly than the one under the human's command.

Through the window, Justin could see the colossal Palace of the Sun against the western sky. Built centuries ago in the most expensive and dazzling shades of marble, it loomed over the command center in its shadow, erected just weeks before by comparison. The elven Viridian dynasty had lived there since before the previous millennium, almost back to the founding of the Argensian Empire. Some of its rulers had never emerged from the large city that the palace comprised. The recent rebellion exposed that dynasty to be demonic, riven with Despair, and overthrew it just a half-year ago. A landless adventurer—a dwarf no less—now sat the Sun Throne. And rumor had it that unless he was issuing a decree or a sentence of judgment, Yula the First never stayed in the palace long. Hansen, the new Commander of the Imperial Array, was Yula's boon companion and member of the adventuring band which had toppled a crown and pushed Justin's family name into disgrace along with it. No matter that hardly any elf suspected the demonic conspiracy; they fought beside Viridian at the Battle of Tor Perite, and when defeated could all have been slain at Yula's order. Justin survived to try and fail at this training course only by the mercy of his former liege's enemy.

But the building kept working its magic on Justin as he continued down to the final turn, the last corridor before the end. The ring of his boots on solid wood, the proud way he saluted passing superiors and the return salute he received, as a comrade, as a peer, filled him with such a burning purpose he could not stay mired in defeat. He had NOT been defeated! Justin knew, his training, his exam answers, his maneuver tests and drills had all been more than adequate. Officers like Trador showed him with their eyes, their attitudes, that he was fit for this life. Some stubborn clerical error persisted, ever since the third week of training. His file mistaken for someone else's, that was all; or perhaps it was intentional. Justin thought at once of Valin.

And like a summoned beast, his nemesis appeared. Down the last hallway, only steps away from the end of Justin's pride, the aquiline face, elegant side-sword and flashing purple cloak of the young lord loomed larger with every jaunty step he took towards him, and doubled with every passionate pace Justin made in return. They met in no time, and Justin kept enough composure to salute a superior as he noted the silver sun-badge on his enemy's shoulders.

"Captain Th'lendor," Justin said, at attention and awaiting the release-return salute. Valin took an extra moment to savor the subservience, then flipped a lazy two-finger tap to his forehead.

"Ah Justin," he drawled, ignoring the cadet's bar across from him, "come to see your final grades." He smirked as he handled the small flag-wrapped pole under one arm. "You can save yourself and Commander Hansen a lot of trouble, you know. Just take the door left of the adjutant's desk, it leads to the wash-out way without bothering Hansen in his office."

"I should have known," Justin replied tightly with his eyes dead ahead, "you would be expert in the shortest and easiest way, Captain."

Valin's face hardened a bit and the smirk slipped. "Not the easiest or shortest way, to the highest marks in the entire cadet class!" This brought Justin's eyes around to search his enemy's gaze. Using the skill he'd learned from his father, Justin drew in Valin's entire demeanor—pace of breath, movement of his pupils, twitches to fingers or tics in the neck—to seek the evidence of a lying tongue. He saw Valin's flare of anger, and the poor self-control that belied the bearing of a truly noble elf; hatred between their families, neighbors and rivals for centuries, insured that. Now, with the varying fortunes of the recent rebellion, one knighthood had fallen, its foef forfeit to the crown while another, betraying its former emperor, basked in the sun. With both fathers slain in the battle, Justin and Valin represented the last hope of their family names. But Valin, whose forefathers had already earned the right to a noble contraction, came perfectly placed to enter the new officer training corps the Emperor created. The death of the elder Th'lendor purchased a spot for his son, while Justin needed to beg and scrape for a last-moment admission.

So Justin saw pent-up anger, and hatred aplenty as usual, behind the mask Valin struggled to maintain. But there was nothing, no sign that Valin had not told the truth with his incredible claim. He had earned the highest marks in the entire corps of cadets, and now strode forth with a banner of mission in hand, while Justin headed to his final doom. For a moment, Justin thought of dropping the pretence. In an hour, he would no longer be bound by the military code; he could hurl an insult, challenge Valin to a duel, earn a measure of satisfaction. But the halls themselves, the sense of purpose they had conveyed since he first stepped inside, forbade it. Then too, his father would have been ashamed.

Mastering himself, Justin saluted again. "Your mission, Captain, is no doubt your affair; I pray Argens Hopeforger will watch over it, and bring the Empire success through you." That was all he could do in answer to his duty; without waiting to be released or for a response, he stepped off at once down the final corridor, hearing Valin's chuckle and the sound of his boots in counterpoint, which he tried to imagine a retreat.

The final hall ended in a small antechamber, holding a central door opposite, a side door to the left whose purpose Justin already knew, and a small desk to the right where the adjutant sat. The man rose at once, and Justin recognized both the face and the officer's brevet. "Dekentar M'nesa Zetee, cadet Justin reporting as ordered."

"Cadet Thyme," the slender elf returned, "I recall well your family; your father was not unknown to my grand-uncle, who spoke well of his character. I regret his death, sir." This kind word, coming from the youngest scion of such a distinguished noble line, formed a most gracious gesture, and Justin bowed his head in recognition before stiffly taking a seat to wait. A stretch of near-silence ensued, underscored by the deep indistinct murmur of the Commander's voice in the office beyond. One more captain being created, Justin thought bitterly to himself. He wondered if he could raise the question of a clerical error without loss of face. No, it wouldn't do—this was the end of his family, no respectable marriage for a line so many times disgraced.

"You seem nervous, sir, if I may make so bold," the dekentar Zetee said, and Justin snapped back from his reverie to check his comportment: he was fiddling with his sword-top making it tap against the wall. "I will not be so free to speak, I am certain, in a few minutes when you outrank me."

"You are most kind, dekentar," Justin managed formally. "In point of fact, I shall be washed out; my grades are the lowest of the corps."

"Lowest for the rank of captain's cadets?" Zetee returned incredulously.

"Lowest for the entire cadre of officers, at any level." Justin rose and drew forth the paper, advancing to hand it over for inspection. The adjutant was already shaking his head, and glanced at it only once.

"This is not correct, sir. I recall well the privilege of serving under you in certain exercises."

"The flanking maneuver, by the ford, yes. I thought we did rather well."

"Our score was perfect, every point the examiners could see to earn, sir. And I can tell you with candor, the other dekentars have related to me opinions similar to my own. We will talk, of an evening."

"Of my family?" Justin challenged with a wry smile.

"Of your performance in command," Zetee admitted. "This score cannot be yours—sir."

"I, well I had suspected perhaps an error of filing…" Justin trailed off when he saw the dekentar's face rise to meet his own.

"I file the grades myself, sir."

"Then I have given insult, and would formally beg—"

"You have given no insult to me, sir," M'nesa was so moved as to interrupt, and Justin's training could see other signs of stress in his character, though partly hidden. "This simply cannot—"

The door opened and an elven noble strode forth, no cadet's bar or any other decoration on his jacket. Without saluting or looking to either side, he strode between the two and through the left-hand door, slamming it behind him. On the heels of the noise came a voice from within that nearly made the furniture vibrate.

"Are there any more, Zetee?"

"One, sir, cadet Justin Thyme to see you."

A short pause, a slight rustle of papers, and then—"Send him in."

Justin retrieved the grading paper and gave M'nesa Zetee a salute, closer and closer to his last, he reflected. The young elf hesitated, then leaned in to speak in low tones of urgency.

"Sir, I cannot understand what has happened to you. Perhaps it would be best to extend my sympathies here. But I would rather—that is, if you would consider…"

"Dekentar?"

"Will you take me on your command, sir? If you should earn one, that is."

Justin was stunned—in truth, a refined and noble officer like Zetee would have been one of his top choices, if he'd had his way. This was an extraordinary compliment, under the circumstances. With a smile, Justin held out his arm and gripped the adjutant's, saying "You honor me sir, and I thank you. If it will please you to hear it, of course I would be happy to have you in my command. But don't wait for me—even elves get old."

Zetee smiled, and gestured to the open door. Justin closed it behind him.

At once, as always, Justin's eye flicked towards Hansen's left arm and the blade affixed to his severed wrist. The human Commander of the Imperial Array, master of more than twelve thousand men now independent of the traditional feudal levy of Argens, loomed well over six feet and bore his full scale armor like an afterthought as he gazed down at his desk. To judge by the rictus across his scarred face, the piled papers there were his real enemy. Justin held his salute until Hansen looked up and returned it. The gaze of Hansen's eyes, one with a crooked scar running over it from outer temple to the bridge of his nose, was always fierce. Since the Commander usually found an excuse to be angry on the training grounds, it was difficult to tell what other emotions, if any, he held, much less how he showed them. More scar-tissue around his naked muscular arms told of warfare and adventure (that word! Even now Justin recoiled a bit to think of the man's former career). He looked on Justin an extra moment, inscrutably—humans were normally so hasty—and then gestured him closer before returning to shuffle his briefs.

One leather wallet open on his desk bore the name "Justin Thyme", full to bursting with thickly marked papers. Hansen rooted about among the other folios buried on his desk, seeking just one amid the throng, and at last withdrew a valise with a name Justin did not see.

"Somehow," Hansen remarked with a tone of fraying patience, "these reports are continually filed in the wrong places." Justin thought of Zetee's remark cut short, and swallowed hard. Perhaps this was his chance.

"Commander, if I may, there has perhaps been—"

"There we are," Hansen interrupted with satisfaction, so like a human to break in. "All papers back where they belong." He inserted the much larger, marked-up notes from Justin's valise to the other, and put in their stead the thin, barely-written comments from the unknown. Thumping Justin's valise to the desk and sitting, Hansen remarked with great emphasis, "That's better. You sir, are washed out."

Justin could think of nothing to say, his mind too full of thoughts and dismay. Fortunately, Hansen had just the words.

"Have a seat, Captain; I have a mission for you."

From his feet, Justin was struggling to frame the haze of his anger into a coherent thought. "I am to understand, then, that some political favor requires … and you have chosen me to bear the disgrace so that—" he stopped himself, as the Commander grinned with impatience, to let the words sink in.

"Did you say—Captain?"

The sun-badge hit the desk hard and bounced up to Justin's chest level, where he caught it by reflex and then sat back heavily in the chair as if its force knocked him down. He felt the sharp points of the silver symbol pressing his palm with a joyous pain, but the haze did not lessen in the least.

"We need a man who hates the Emperor, who wants him to fail and fall, up in the North Mark where everyone feels the same way."

"You said—washed out, sir?"

"Of course. Am I going too fast for you, Captain?"

Hansen opened Justin's valise and took out papers, gazing at them in a way that said he knew he was being watched. He looked up at Justin, "It says here you have the ability to discern lies from truth." Galvanized, Justin dared to take in everything about the Commander's appearance in the moment after he spoke; drawing a sharp breath, he replied, "No, it doesn't."

"Eh?" said Hansen, honestly surprised, "what do you mean?"

"You do have that report, sir, and it is accurate. But it's not in those papers there. That report is back in the stack," Justin said in a tone that leaked some anger despite his best efforts, "and I would respectfully request that I be allowed to review it."

"Oh, I see." Hansen replied, with relief. "No, that won't be necessary. I can recall anything needful—ask me."

"You, sir? My scores—"

"Highest in the corps, any level, any phase. Try a tough one."

"Highest? I don't understand—you mean, the error—"

"There's no error. I swapped the papers," Hansen replied imperturbably. "Several times," he added with a look out the door to where the adjutant sat. "Meddling little know-it-all, wish someone would take him off my hands."

Hansen leaned in to speak with clarity. "You demonstrate an excellent understanding of the tactical and strategic principles we have laid down in this course, Captain. If you don't die in the next month, you could command a brigade of any size under me, as far as I'm concerned. Your equestrian skills are the finest our Master of Horse has ever seen—and I gather he's four times as old as me, though you elves are always so touchy when asked about your age. You undertook a night maneuver with your pentadek, given the slightest latitude, that not only succeeded, it brought the exercise to a close twelve hours earlier than we had anticipated."

"I recall that exercise, sir. I was assigned back to remedial physical training—"

"Yes," Hansen crested over him with something like anger, "so we could take the rest of the corps and show them what you had done! And to pretend we had always known, damn you. Your sense of how to exploit the exposed flank of an enemy, even when it is interior, is not without risks. But it was something our trainers had never considered."

If Justin had not already been sitting he would have fallen down. His head was whirling as if he flew at a great height. He swallowed uselessly and tried to compose his thoughts. Every time he had performed under command in training, it felt right to him; whenever he saw his scores afterwards, he tried his best to see how he could have been wrong. Now, he found his first instincts justified, perhaps beyond his own ambition. He stared down at the captain's sun in his hand, still gripping it as if it might drop out of his life altogether.

"You—spoke of a mission, sir."

Hansen rose and motioned Justin over to the map on the wall. From the capital Argens, on the central west coast of the empire, Justin could already see the precious parchment had been marked with notes, arrows, the sketch of potential future campaigns. With the Empire at peace barely half a year, those marks wounded the lands they represented. To the North Mark were several arrows denoting lines of advance, potential locations of supply depots, and much more in crabbed, handwritten notes. Justin scanned the marks and realized the vision of a ruinous civil war they represented, the cost in flame and blood. It chilled him to think of this long-rumored possibility, even as he felt a thrill to be let in on such secrets. He stared sidelong at Hansen with wonder—if the Commander was aware of the gift of trust he gave, he showed no sign.

"These bastards in the north," he grated, "have a long history of rising against imperial authority. Only the Viridian emperors kept them down—and now we're beginning to see why. The power of a demon on the throne, and the lore they passed down through those damned Demonbender preachers of theirs, worked for a few centuries to the advantage of the Overlord, as they call the North Mark in Cryssigens. Rumor is there's a demon under the palace, restrained only by the power of the ruler himself. Now, with that power broken, the sect in ruins, and a new dynasty here—if you want to call it that!—well, revolt is in their blood and they don't need an excuse. Argens' Balls, Yula killed Overlord Kreel himself, to start the rebellion, right there in the arena of Cryssigens. New Year's day 2001, at the great games. Yula fought his way to the main stand and slew him right in the viewing box. Eighty thousand people in the stands saw it! Wish I'd had time to watch, but there was this elephant running loose," and the Commander's grin was fond. "Then his son falls too, six months later at the Battle of Tor Perite, where we finally broke Viridian's power. Two Marks slain in less than half a year, no children left, no inheritance for the seat of the Overlord. That was the summer of 2001. You can just imagine how popular our new emperor Yula is across the North Mark today."

Hansen gestured with the blade-end of his left arm as he spoke, his remaining right hand clenched in a fist nearly all the time. Justin could read the barely contained fury in his tone and began to wonder, with a sinking feeling, why the invasion had not already been launched. "The lords of the Mark will be meeting soon, to choose a new successor—" Justin began, but again the human interrupted him.

"To pick a new leader for their uprising, you mean! The Emperor must be represented at that table, Justin, it's vital. These bastards, left to themselves, would try to resurrect the worship of Argens Demonbender, bring back slavery, the drug trade, all the rest of it. And it would mean a civil war. I will leave every house in the North Mark on fire before I let this kingdom go one step back towards that." He noticed Justin watching him instead of the map, and turned away a bit calmer. "I have no deep religious convictions myself—I was raised in the northern lands, followed Areghel. I've learned to fight and fight well—none of us, truth to tell, really had any idea how far our adventuring would take us. Pretty damn far!" He spun back and looked the elven knight's-son in the eye. "It's really Morinack, he's the planner, I'll tell you honestly. Yula asks us all to speak, but he knows I'm just the weapon, not the guiding mind. But what we're building here—men need to be free, damn Viridian and the poison he poured over this Empire for centuries. I won't see it lost by a bunch of strut-proud noble fools who think they're too good for us and look for another war at the first excuse. It's the policy, can't they see that?"

Justin straightened and said, "Of course they will, sir. I can see it now—it's why I signed up."

"I need you Justin, to be the Emperor's eyes and ears in Cryssigens."

Justin's mouth opened some moments before he could speak. "I—I will of course be honored to carry the Emperor's banner to the conference table—"

"What? Hell packed with demons, no! You're not going there with the banner, you're a washout, remember?" Hansen sounded angry, but he laughed out loud at the rare sight of Justin's dumbfounded look. Stepping over to clap him hard on the back, he said, "Perhaps I've put things into the wrong order. Sit and let me explain."

"The banner of the Emperor's official mission is already assigned—not to you, I'm no waster of talent. To someone who—well, let us just say, someone nobly placed and believable as a boot-licker of the Emperor's side."

Justin caught his breath. "A noble elf, with a contracted name? Whose father died fighting for the rebellion?"

Hansen's grin was feral as he opened the file with Justin's name on it and looked over the papers within. "Let's see ... rides a horse well enough. I have here a note that he can yell 'charge!' very clearly. As for the rest—Areghel's Crown, what an idiot ... let us say we have dispatched a man very fit for the job, and at the head of a centar of cavalry-with remounts, nice uniforms, all that. He is empowered to insist on the traditional right of the Emperor to have a voice in the deliberations over the choosing of the next Overlord of the North Mark. And since any motion for an immediate vote of succession must be unanimous, the Emperor's voice at that table will ensure a delay. Meanwhile, our official envoy will do his job, which is to give the conspirators of the North Mark no reason to suspect that we are up to anything more important than posing and insisting."

"Valin," Justin breathed, his heart trying to pull in five directions at once. "Valin T'lenthor, at the head of a full centar of mounted men. Sir, they will love to hate him."

"And that hate won't be wasted, when he uses his authority to demand a delay in the usurper's name. Ten more weeks, as long as he can reach their council before the ides of this month. Two months, in which he thinks he will be waiting for further instructions from me."

"When in truth, sir?"

"I will be awaiting instructions from you. You are to march two dekents north to the Mark and pose as a mercenary looking for a side to take. Get people talking, find out who we can trust. And make contact with our agent there. You'll find out from her how to get safe messages back to me here."

Hansen reached into the desk drawer and took out a small ring with the symbol of an axe-blade, so stylized it looked like a geometric decoration. "This is the signet of the agent in Cryssigens you'll make contact with. That's all I know," and here he stopped to distinctly pronounce a curse that Justin had never heard in his life. "Milord Morinack, the new Emperor's Hand, is in charge of the intelligence corps," he muttered "and he does not see fit to share his intelligence with the military. But he says you'll have no trouble. All the times I saved his tiny behind ... evidently she's a woman, so you've got it narrowed down by nearly half already."

Justin donned the ring on his smallest finger, and took a deep breath trying to think of other questions he should ask.

"How do I explain the captain's badge?"

Hansen shrugged. "You need to have the obedience of the men you hire. I'll let the word out that a few badges have been, ah, purchased, you can pretend your last silver piece went into it. Officially, the badge gives you authority to order the men, they might snigger but they'll have to accept it. I'm sure you can prove yourself to them—you have to me. And, well, I owed you something for the carking I'm giving you otherwise. I need someone exactly like you, Justin—your family was ruined in the war," here he paused and for the first time seemed almost apologetic, "which was rough on a lot of people, of course. You were there at Tor Perite, where this empire suffered the loss of two thousand knights and twice as many soldiers. I commanded the forces of the rebellion," Hansen said, standing straight, "If any man is responsible for your capture, the death of your father, it's me. Comment?"

"Yours was the victory, Commander, by your force of arms and superior strategy. I feel no shame in defeat, only in the association of my former lords, which neither my father nor any of us suspected."

"I know that. I sense you are loyal to this new cause. It's bigger than me, or Yula, or any of us. But listen to me, Captain," and here the commander leaned in and dropped his voice to a lethal level. "You have seen the beginnings of what this new strategy can do. I now have a cadre of officers and men nearly three thousand strong. Thirty centars trained to understand these principles, do you mark me, sir? In the North Mark, it's still a feudal army," Hansen's voice curdled with disdain, "lords with lances, mobs of metal men on horseback who race to be the first, the idea that courage is genius."

Hansen sat back slowly, and his voice was dropping to a whetstone whisper. "At Tor Perite, less than a third of the Empire's feudal levy defected. Even with our north-kingdom allies, we were outnumbered more than four to three. If the North Mark rebels, I will bring the rest of the Empire's knights, plus every man-jack of this new corps against these demon-kissing rebels. This will not be a fair fight, Justin—I will bury their noble class to the last man. The North Mark will be ruled by women and children for the next twenty years, and its principal export will be smoke. And that responsibility, Captain, is on you."

Hansen rose and strode to the back of the office. "You came to this program for a new start, and I believe you've made the best of it. Well, this is the best I can offer you. Damn few men, no reputation or glory, just a chance to run into the hottest fire burning in this empire and try to put it out with your bare hands. You're washed out as soon as you leave this office. And you're the best officer of this first class of cadets. I need you, damn their hides" this last to the map, as if the North Mark could hear him, or would care.

Justin thought as quickly as he could. He had so badly hungered to restore his name, and had received instead, at best, anonymity. But Hansen would know the truth. And Argens. It would have to be enough. "May I choose my own dekentars?"

"Any that are left. For men, only those the other Captains leave behind, I'm afraid. We can't let you compete for them, or the horses. And no remounts—you need to look poor."

Justin smiled. "I will, sir. Destitute."

Hansen half-reached to salute, but stopped and made a decision He turned to the back wall and opened a chest. "I want you to have this, Justin. It isn't that it's much, just that—damn! I'm sending you into the sewer, and it makes me want to chew wood. Here," thrusting a helmet at him roughly. Justin took the helm, silver-chased with the device of a bird of prey; the wings swept back past his ears and in the beak above the forehead was a small well-cut emerald. Justin gazed on it, as fine a piece as anything Valin ever wore, boldly executed but tasteful.

"I wore it in my early days, in the north. When I was free. It carries a spell of protection, nothing too puissant. But perhaps it will bring you luck. And there's no need to look completely destitute," he finished with a smile of his own.

Justin tore his eyes from the green gem and the glare of the hawk, tucking the helm under his arm and giving his salute. "I am in your debt, commander."

"Day-old shit, you've been carked and we both know it. Let me hear from you as soon as you make contact. Try to stay on the right side of the history that's being made. That is all. Captain." Hansen saluted with a wry grimace, followed by a shushing motion with his sword-hand to his lips. Justin snapped off his best salute and turned to go.

In the outer office, he saw M'nesa Zetee putting the final papers into his desk and locking the drawer with a key he left on its top.

"You heard?"

"Enough," the dekentar smiled back. "The third time your grades were filed wrong, I knew it was no mistake. I admire the Commander, but I quit."

The two left the office by the wash-out door, and Justin heard the ring of his boots turn from wooden purpose to stone, and deed. Only then did he don the helm and the captain's badge of office. He looked at the coveted prize he'd thought never to have, then to Zetee who saluted his new commanding officer.

"How do I look?" Justin asked.

"Like a commander of soldiers, Captain." Zetee looked to the badge and became puzzled, thinking this through.

"I bought it," Justin supplied.

"It looks very well on you, sir."

"Let's go put together a company, dekentar. We have less than two weeks to get to Cryssigens."

Interlude:

The demon sits in silence, every once so often reaching with its mind to test the barriers. For fourteen centuries the result has never changed; its bonds made of glassteel walls, spells and inscribed circles still hold, are still adequate. But ever so slightly, they weaken. The dimensions of its subterranean prison are large, cold, and completely dark. What need of anything a breather would want, when so few have made the difficult trip past guards and wards to visit it? And consideration of the demon's needs has never been a priority.

Overhead, the creature can sense three furlongs of stone, the underpinning of the Crystal Palace of the city of Cryssigens, home to its mortal leader. So long has the demon been held here, the breathers believe their castle, their city might come crashing down in fire should it escape. Now the Overlord has died, and none replaces him. Again the demon contemplates what satisfaction that day would bring. But the walls hold, for now.

"You seek to escape, demon." The voice from a distant corner of its black world is the first heard here in many years, and the prisoner does not bother to conceal its surprise. At once, it reaches out to read the mind of its guest, bemused that the passing of time made it sleep through the arrival.

"But you cannot, not yet," the voice continues, its echoes destroying any sense of age or gender, but retaining a tone of confidence and the love of risk. "The city is yet safe from the Shard Demon, but all say the wards of your prison are coming unset. How long do we have, can you tell me?"

The creature shifts slightly, just enough to indicate interest. The scraping joints annihilate any other sounds across the cavern, creating sparks of fire that streak the blind-black around it. The visitor lurks in shadows far away, but the demon keeps groping with its mind. Not seeking to recognize a face, the monster quests instead to gauge the power of this interloper. Some signs of the needed ability are there—and then a blank wall, further proof of the mortal's lore and potential usefulness.

"How long do we have?" the voice inquires again, and with a sense of gleeful wonder, the demon realizes its mind, too, is being searched. Amazed and delighted, it allows the mortal inside, giving it a guided tour of selected rooms and slapping thought-fingers away from doors not germane to its own purposes. Young, easily handled, but nimble it thinks. For a moment the Shard Demon wonders if there would be a test of wills, here for the first time in centuries. Perhaps it should lose, just this once. But the mind withdraws.

"As I thought," the voice murmurs to itself, and try as it might the demon in prison cannot discern that thought. "Everywhere, I see 'perhaps' … perhaps you will try harder to break free. Perhaps there will be a new Mark before you can do so," and this statement chills the air around the demon already cold as crystal. The voice seems to smile. "Yet perhaps … you will break free, before a new lord can be chosen to master you. The votes of the council might be delayed. Perhaps you will loose your bonds and bring chaos to the lands … with assistance."

Lurching to its feet the demon slams its gem-hard fists against the glassteel in a cacophony of screeches, from its knees, shoulders and throat. The sparks explode in all directions and light the cavern to its edges—showing only empty space. The merest echo of a laugh survives the exit of the intruder. So—somewhat more powerful than first appearances, this visitor. Powerful enough to master its will, command wishes, or free it to destroy the entire kingdom? Perhaps. With a chuckle that spits embers, the Shard Demon sits again, and returns to waiting a while longer.

$$\oplus \ \oplus \ \oplus$$

Justin and M'nesa moved across the back of the compound, but ignored the exit gate, heading the long way around to where the subalterns and soldiers quartered. The noon brilliant sun and the winter weather, when the Southlands approached its coolest, held at that perfect level no man of action could complain of. Exercise still triggered sweat, but it dried quickly and there was just a hint of a spur to keep moving. Justin needed no urging; now that he had a mission, the more he could keep busy the less he had to think about his slim chances for success. But if his mission was to jump into a lava-crack and search for hell, he could not have been disappointed—against all expectations he was a captain of men, and under orders to the empire.

He and M'nesa conferred hurriedly as to their cover story and were ready before they came within earshot of the dekentars. Only a few missions had been assigned this morning—various tasks such as Valin's—so well over a score of subalterns were standing about trading jests or sword-feints when M'nesa addressed them.

"Dekentars, my captain has a mission. We need an officer to command the second dekent, and the interviews will take place…" checking back to Justin, who pointed to an angle of the barrier fence, "over there."

Every soldier came along to stand for the job, if only from boredom. For the first few steps the following dekentars could see Justin's back, and the helm hid his head. When he turned and they saw his face, six or more slowed at once, found some lame distraction to turn their steps, or just reversed course without excuse. Justin took no umbrage from that, nor a few minutes later, when he had interviewed most of them in turn and found that several more had walked out after his first question.

The manual for officers choosing subalterns gave guidance that a small number of questions should be asked. Each candidate should answer the same ones as the others, and reluctance to answer, or insistence from the questioner, were both frowned upon. Question and answer each deserved their own respect. This was the kind of thing Justin had spent many an hour devising—fruitlessly, he had thought—and he showed no hesitation now.

"I have only two questions, dekentar Mailnim," he said crisply to the fourteenth candidate, standing at attention. Justin stood four feet away with his back to the barrier, and M'nesa unobtrusively listened in to one side.

"What is your age?" Justin watched the young elf's face move from discomfort to outright shock. No noble elf in his right mind would tell another being his age, outside his family who already knew. If a Man or Dwarf had asked, it would be justification for a physical beating; from another elf, even if nobly born, it was rude in the extreme. Justin could already tell this one was younger than he, his mouth gaping like a fish and three full breaths before he could say anything.

"You dare—you ask that of me!"

"You think this job will not require daring, soldier?"

"You may insult my courage if you wish, sir. But I have no desire to sully my reputation by further conversation. Good day." Forgetting to salute, he spun on his heel and retired in a dudgeon beyond his years.

"Not the best answer we've heard so far," M'nesa remarked.

"Better than any of the six who lied," Justin shot back casually, which brought his subaltern's head around. "I only have a few moments to decide, M'nesa, I cannot afford the niceties." Gesturing to the next man, Justin saw the large human he'd seen before; behind him was only one more candidate, Kein Trador. Justin smiled at the thought of that man, but suppressed his eagerness so that he could do his duty. The human marched up smartly enough and saluted properly, though his grin never really disappeared.

"Tass, captain."

"No last name?" M'nesa asked, and was favored with a grin in return.

"Needed none, in the arena. Sir."

So—Justin looked over the man's neck and sandaled feet thick with scars, and the evidence of a broken nose across his face. A former gladiator; there had been rumors that Hansen admitted candidates based on merit as well as birth, and of course a few soldiers who were once slaves bolstered the new policy. But an officer—no wonder the man had not yet been assigned.

"What is your age?"

Tass barked a laugh and did not hesitate. "I'm thirty-four." Such candor was refreshing, though Justin reflected the mortal had already lived half his years. Moving to the next question, he definitely expected a pause before an answer.

"And what, sir, is your Hope?" But once again the subaltern surprised him.

"Not to see forty."

"How is that?"

"The only interest I've ever had, is when I've risked my life. The games, the crowd sees the thrilling part—truth is, there's a lot of pissing and waiting, and you can only practice so much before you're perfect, like me. I've been here three months since the war, and it's pretty much the same. Food's worse. I want out! See some real action—the only kind I've known, besides the occasional woman. Wouldn't mind dying in either place!" Here he laughed full and long, and Justin could see his missing teeth. "But either way, I won't be good for much in a few years. I want to make the most of them. Sir" he added with a salute for punctuation.

"I am very pleased to have met you, dekentar," Justin said covering the urge to smile. "If you would just wait with the others—"

"Yes, sir," Tass drawled, turning to go. M'nesa put in another word, "You fought in the arena? Where, if it's not prying."

"Prying! Balls of Argens you're polite. The only arena worth mentioning, of course—Cryssigens. Three years, twenty fights to the death, and the record—you see me standing here?" He proudly pointed to himself as prime evidence. "I fought next to Kallisthenes, same team," he added, naming the man who drew shivers from every elf that had fought under Viridian. Yula had helped that reaver break free, with his gladiator gang, and they fought their way in a fiery path across the Mark, the beginning of the rebellion just over a year ago. Now elevated to high command, Kallisthenes took the authority of Yula the Usurper with him, and an enormous crowd of freedmen, ruined retainers and ambitious hangers-on, to repopulate the lost Far Mark across the desert to the east. If right-thinking elves could judge any of Yula's deeds worthy, getting the living bogeyman out of the empire proper would be it. M'nesa looked thoughtful as Tass returned to the group and his loud jests, while Kein Trador stepped smartly up.

"Dekentar Kein Trador, you wished me well earlier today, and I think your desires have wrought to my benefit."

"If the captain will recall, it was to myself that I wished good luck, sir." Trador exchanged a grin with M'nesa that seemed familiar and Justin noted it.

"How old are you, dekentar?"

The shock was enough to wipe the smile off the elf's face, and for a moment he looked away to M'nesa as if for inspiration. Finding none, he considered a time, and Justin saw dismay and uncertainty, but no determination to hide or show insult. After a moment, his face lit up and the candidate responded, "In truth, sir, I am almost precisely a half-year older than Dekentar Zetee!"

M'nesa laughed in surprise at that, and said, "It's the truth, captain" and Justin nodded, reminding him, "I know."

"Deftly turned, Trador. The best answer I have heard today, in fact." The young elf had made it a question that needed to be asked of his peer, and Justin could not move another step without revealing whether he had, in fact, asked him. A nice demonstration of the need for equity among his command.

"And what, Kein Trador, is your Hope?"

The second question, though also personal, was not nearly so delicate. But it raised the issue of a person's essential philosophy, and in the aftermath of the rebellion had gained a lot of currency. All Argensians were horrified to realize that the emperor Viridian was nothing more than a demon in disguise, and the overthrow of established orders, such as the guild of slavers and the sect of Argens Demonbender, had ruined careers and shattered fortunes. Everywhere, citizens were asking what, if anything, they truly believed in, and what made a man a Child of Hope. Kein Trador could not claim to be surprised by this question, though he might still be unsure how to answer.

He closed his eyes for a moment in thought. "I hope that within two years, I should be Captain of the array," he said steadily with a soldier's grin. His smile faded, and he added with quiet sincerity, "and receiving my orders from strategos Thyme." M'nesa gave a chortle that spoke of familiarity with this sort of talk, but Justin saw no hint of the lie or even of exaggeration in the straight gaze Trador returned to him. He had answered philosophy with action, and claimed that his hope would be the same as Justin's. From a human, such words could be dismissed as flattery. But this fellow was of noble elven descent, and most likely a near-neighbor of Zetee. Justin nodded and saluted the subaltern away; as Kein retreated to the others, he noticed M'nesa's fond smile dying in a way that troubled him.

An instinct nudged, and Justin paused at the edge of his first command decision. Though his heart misgave him, he knew he had to ask. "M'nesa, what is your opinion—who should be the second subaltern?"

The face he saw was tight as a drum, and M'nesa managed, "Sir—it must be Tass."

"What! Are you serious?"

M'nesa calmly put his hands behind his back as they discussed in private under the shade of the barrier. A trumpet sounded on the other side of the compound where the soldiers quartered and armed. A detachment was forming up to leave, and all the waiting dekentars looked in that direction.

"You should not fear that merit marches with favoritism here."

"Sir, I do not," M'nesa's face was plainly in pain. He said again, only "Tass".

"Kein Trador is an excellent horseman."

"As are you, sir. Even I am passable," M'nesa said with a shadow of a grin. "You will command two dekents. One must be of foot."

"Oh? Why so?" Justin challenged.

"We will have no remounts, sir. The single horse of each man must be walked for at least part of the time on march. And losses to the horses will be more difficult to replace. So we will for all effects be marching hardly faster than infantry. We don't know the challenges we will face—we must have the advantage of combined arms."

The captain could see the force of this at once. When he had dreamed of command, Justin like most of his fellows had overdone it—extra horses, plenty of cavalry, supply wagons rolling in the background. He even knew which stallion he wanted to pick out—his knight's heritage would not die after a few months of training. But M'nesa was speaking sense.

"Still—why not Trador?" he challenged to draw his officer out.

"We need a dekentar of foot, to make up for our deficiencies."

"You think elves will follow a man?"

"Better than an elf on a horse—excepting you of course, sir. The infantry dekent will need a leader who is of them. Tass is ... most puissant," M'nesa finished with the phrase Justin would likely have chosen as well. But he had to know where the youngest Zetee stood; perhaps he needed to answer questions like the others.

"There are immortal soldiers who would never consent to follow a human. What if I put him in command of you?"

M'nesa looked up sharply but with those calm features painted in place. "Then it will have been you, sir, who gave the order. My father had humans among his peasants, said they were like children who never grow up. Then he would set his hands to his waist and wonder aloud if we would ever become elves—very witty."

"Captain, the new Empire has no room in it for those who would place one race permanently above another. Perhaps you've noticed, who now sits the Throne of the Sun?" He allowed himself a smile, then added, "I could live a thousand years if I stayed huddled in a corner all day and had a servant bring me food. We are soldiers, sir, all of us. Under command to the empire, any of us could die tomorrow. What difference, then, how long we could have lived?"

Justin was pleased to see his instinct so well borne out. He baited Zetee one last time, on a different tack.

"But—Trador is of such noble family."

"Sir!" M'nesa's expression now was anguished, "are you arguing for or against? We go into hostile territory on a secret mission. We must not draw undue attention. Your family has been ruined. I am the youngest of four, quite rare, and I doubt anyone's heard the name of Zetee in the North Mark. But three noble sons, in a company supposedly disgraced? Sir, Tass is from Cryssigens—he knows the city, the customs. Which of us would you send into a tavern to get the lay of the land?"

Justin recognized the power of his subaltern's logic, though it hurt him sorely to lose Trador. His composure slipped a moment, and he said, "But—he is your friend."

The admission allowed M'nesa to regain some of his possession: he looked directly ahead and replied, "Since infancy, sir. If it would please the captain, I will bring him the news myself."

With his heart heavy inside him, Justin gave just an echo of a nod, and M'nesa spun heels to withdraw. The loss of Trador bit Justin hard, but the order was clear. Even twenty men might be pushing things, once he arrived in Cryssigens—he needed to look minor, unimportant, just useful.

But as the brash human sauntered over to salute again and shake his hand, Justin found he simply could not transfer any resentment to his new recruit. Tass greeted each piece of information in his briefing as humorous—though he clearly understood the nature of the mission, his grin just grew. "We'll be hip-deep in crap, is what you're saying sir," he rasped, and then laughed out loud. "Finally. I was falling asleep toward the end of training."

"Have you each given thought how to recruit your dekents?" Justin asked as they walked past the subalterns and towards the soldier compound. M'nesa said a few things about horsemanship tests and a set of questions, which seemed in good sense. Tass merely clenched his fists with dancing eyes, like a hungry guard dog eager to be unleashed.

At the entry gate, they had to stop as a parade of men was marching out; eight dekents of horse and two of foot, led by Valin bearing the flag of mission. Several hundred gathered along the route to the compound gate, to watch this first mission depart. Most of the men and officers, not assigned a special command, would return to training after today. They watched the departing company with undisguised envy. M'nesa scanned the horsemen for faces he recalled, and moaned quietly when he saw the accoutrements of the company.

"Look you—remounts, two supply wagons with tents, there's even a trumpeter."

On Justin's other side, Tass slid a bored gaze over the whole lot like some painting he didn't care to buy. "Lily-flowers," he muttered, "hope they need a parade wherever they're going. And cark me! look, the idiot made sure all his infantry are the same height!"

Justin saw only the magnificent auburn stallion between his rival's legs and quietly swore. "Flame of the First, the bastard took Sirocco." Without question, Valin T'lenthor cut a splendid figure sitting nearly sixteen hands high in the cruppers of that powerful beast. It was sired, they said, in the emperor's personal stables and had seen action in five pitched battles, never throwing its rider. Now it bobbed its head and snorted with joyous impatience to be back in harness and hearing the sound of metal on all sides. Justin had the presence of mind to shrug his cape down over the badge.

Valin, reining in before the trio, ignored Justin and instead addressed M'nesa.

"The Commander's adjutant surely has better ways to spend an afternoon than moping about with mortals and civilians." Stiffening, M'nesa contented himself with cutting his salute a little short, while Justin thought of five witty retorts and gave none of them. But Tass walked a different path. Turning to Justin he asked, "You want me to get this horse for you sir?"

The implied treason was, in itself, a statement of loyalty. Valin took the human seriously and started back in his seat, causing Sirocco to rear slightly and miss a few steps. M'nesa, catching the mood, put in, "Careful there, show some control." Tass looked across to his peer and said, "I'm just a poor foot soldier, sir, tell me—which one were you talking to?" Valin's sneer wrinkled, and his disdainful laughter cracked just a bit, as he needlessly gestured to his dekentars to lead the men out by the gate.

The ring of thirty-score hooves on the stone streets stopped all activity until the company had passed from view. Everything Justin had dreamed of gave back dimmer echoes for a long time—as his men waited the shadow-officer stood still and listened, silently saying goodbye.

"Captain?" M'nesa gently prompted, and Justin stirred as if from sleep.

"Let us recruit the men."

The common soldiers trained, ate and slept in a separate section of the compound from the officers. Rigorous physical testing had sifted out more than four of every five candidates, back at the start of the training course; others washed out for poor temper or inadequate discipline, and the rest had become quite used to harsh schedules, unfair conditions and surprise tests. Justin felt lonely as he approached with just his two subalterns to the ground where hundreds of them lounged, waiting for the midday meal. As long as he saw entire centars of men as a group, it was intimidating. But coming closer, Justin began to pick out individuals: that tall one who fell in the river, the blonde who fought on with his fists when disarmed, the laughing pair who must be brothers he met on the first day. He recognized single men, and their numbers became unimportant: they recognized him, and the situation clarified even further. They were already sorting themselves out by the time M'nesa announced the mission and the number needed.

"Those who wish to stand for the cavalry dekent, will meet me by the stables. For the foot, here with Tass. Captain, will you accompany me?"

Justin shook his head, "I know how you'll do it, and trust you'll come back with the ten best. Horses, as well as men; and one for me if you would. I wish to observe our new dekentar."

M'nesa moved off with several dozen men in tow, and a loose semi-circle of over eighty men formed around Justin and Tass. "So, Captain," one fellow called, almost taunting, "what's it to be?"

Justin tilted his head towards Tass, who had retrieved two shields and two wooden swords from the tilt-rack. With a tiny grin, the hulking human tossed down one pair and donned the second.

Facing them, Tass said simply, "Touch me."

The taunting fellow cried, "What, no examination? Can't you think of any questions?" The group buzzed with muttered jokes, but the dekentar showed no sign.

"I can think of one, the only one I'm interested in," Tass replied, and his grin grew just a slice. "Can any man-jack of you delicate daughters touch me?"

The catcalls and insults died out in an instant, and there wasn't a sound from the entire compound. Stepping forward, Tass wedged a foot under the practice sword and lightly flipped it at his first candidate, the taunter who caught it on reflex. Tass advanced until he was less than three feet away, and spread his arms wide to leave a target. "You do know what a touch is?"

With a snarl, the soldier gripped his weapon and arced it down right at the joint between Tass's neck and shoulder. But Tass had already taken a turning step away, causing the sweep to miss by inches as he gave the man his back. Still with arms wide, he called out to the rest, "I mean, you ARE soldiers, aren't you? Or does living forever mean you put off everything?"

As his attacker came on to his unprotected back, Tass casually stomped on the unused shield, flipping it up to grab with his shield-hand. He turned, deflecting the second attack as if by accident, and held out the shield to his foe. The furious elf batted it aside and swung again—the blow came down solidly on the front of Tass' chest with a resounding "thwak!" Looking slowly down at the enormous red welt, Tass said "ow" in a gentle tone, then looked back up with his widening grin. "Good, soldier, good. Now put that shield on. And hit me again before I hit you three times."

The taunter did not. Nor did the next elf after him. By the time the fourth candidate was trying, and failing, the semi-circle of men around Tass and Justin had thinned considerably. Two men hit Tass once before the third hit on themselves, and these he put to one side along with several others who had not scored. One, after trying repeatedly without success, threw down his arms and turned away cursing that he wouldn't waste his time serving under a human. Tass calmly stepped up and drove a crushing blow across his shoulder-blade that knocked him down. As the men stepped back with oaths, Tass leaned down to the elf moaning in the dirt. "Yes," he whispered gaily, "that is broken. While you're healing up, think on how you washed out, and do better next time, or go back to selling groceries."

Wheeling to the circle around him, the subaltern roared in an enormous voice, one Justin could imagine ringing in the arena. "I hit him from behind! Can you believe it? What sort of job is this! Why, a man could get hurt—a MAN could get hurt, if any elf can be found who can lay a sword on him." From that moment, the soldiers subtly settled into two groups—two of every remaining three, who stood back determined to watch, and the few who now crowded forward to take him on. Tass's grin looked like it might split his face, and he held his weapons wider and wider apart as if his chest, his fearsome reach, his vitality itself would fight for him. Justin realized the man was very good in a fight—not merely fast, but without a split second of indecision about what to do. Perhaps he leaned too hard on the counter-stroke, which could leave him vulnerable to a feint. With a shock, Justin realized he was considering taking the man on. Tass's thirst for combat was infectious.

The sound of approaching hoofbeats and the casual chatter of voices pulled him around. M'nesa had quickly settled his choices and led a dekent of cavalry to one side of the training ground where Tass was culling the recruits. Justin turned to take them in a moment, and could see at once that M'nesa had the beginnings of a unit. Directing them by the hand-signals they had all learned in training, he turned them by caracole so that the line faced the infantry; putting them at ease, he bantered casually as they watched the bouting, cheering for good hits and catcalling bad misses. M'nesa called each one by surname, and clearly had studied the families of the empire to know this or that about several.

In one hand he led a dappled mare already saddled for Justin. The captain moved to inspect her and while the color and size did not impress, he came to see M'nesa had made an excellent choice. Good bones, a very strong chest, in the prime of age, and when he looked the mare in the eye he saw steadiness. "Her name is Furta," the dekentar said with a smile, and Justin chuckled at the elven word. "Can you?" he asked the mare, "can you keep a secret, then?" The horse seemed to nod at just the right time, and Justin clapped her on the neck before swinging up to the saddle.

On the trial-ground, the last of the elven soldiers was taking every measure to break past Tass' guard, with obvious skill but without success. The human wasn't even attacking anymore, just blocking and shifting, taking the measure of the recruit. Still no progress—Tass dropped his shield but did not swing to a fencer's stance, leaving his side exposed. The elf attacked thrice more, each one parried by a strong arm that staggered him; finally the candidate crouched back to simply wait. Tass held a few moments more, gesturing his opponent in; when there was no response, he dropped his sword and stood there defenceless. That was too much—the soldier charged in swinging. Tass stepped up, took the shield on one shoulder without giving ground and caught the sword-wrist in one hand. Grasping the man's midriff with the other, Tass clenched him tight as a lover, grinned hugely in the man's face, and then lifted him a foot clean off the ground before throwing him down. Stunned, the elf rolled slowly to his feet and groped after his dropped sword; he seemed unused to this style of combat, but very game to keep trying. Tass held up one hand and gestured for him to join the success-line.

As luck would have it, that made ten. Justin looked them over, and saw nothing of pattern in the dekent. Some were tall, some broad, two were quite old, one as ugly a man as the captain had ever seen. Most were dirty after bouting with Tass, and the last one on the end was filthy, dusting himself off in a small cloud that obscured the view. Tass took his position at the line's near end and saluted. "My dekent, captain. I'm sure they all have names."

Justin rode the line wondering what his subaltern's method had produced for him. But all such considerations were swept away when he came to the end. Dismounting in haste, he landed before the last soldier, still covered in dirt but standing straight and saluting. On his uniform shoulder there were tiny rips where dekentar's brevets had been fixed; and in his shield hand the elf held the metal bars tightly and almost out of sight.

"Dekentar Trador, what are—"

"Just a common soldier, captain."

Justin stood still and looked him in the eye a long moment. That a noble's son would actually be willing to accept demotion, to walk instead of ride in order to be in his company, was a gesture that made his throat tighten. But discipline would have to be observed. Justin held out his hand, saying roughly, "I have but two dekentars under my command."

At once Trador gave over the brevets and nodded. "Yes sir."

"Of course, the day may come."

"The day may come, sir."

Tass moseyed down the line and caught the conversation. "We'll be very pleased," he leered, "to have this noble young man in our company, I assure you sir." Justin saw clearly the scut-work and pranks that were in store, but turned on his heel to remount. This dekent belonged to his officer. Trador would earn his keep.

By mid-afternoon the small company was possessed of weapons, rations and all the necessary supplies they could carry. Yet Justin waited until full dark before he led out a much smaller procession than Valin's, no trumpet, no thunder of hooves or wheels. But his company, all the same.

⊕ ⊕ ⊕

Try and tell Skeer Two-Eye to his face that he's afraid; he'd laugh and gut you in the same moment. But he hated hearing messages from his master—the lesser demon in his cave required a death to make the voice come through across the leagues from the capital city of the Mark. Yet the moons were up and it was the night for his status report.

The men dragged another peasant into the cave—the last of the logger's family, or the first of the gleaner's? Skeer didn't waste a glance at the face to be sure. Grasping his battle-axe high up on the haft, the reaver crouched over the place where they held the victim prone—already deeply gagged so as not to drown out the conversation—and made a pendulum cut across the sternum. Wide and shallow, it bled like a stream, running back off the neck and down the stone-cut channel they'd made, leading to the iron cage. The three-legged thing inside, just taller than a hunting dog, groped blindly to where the pool of blood trickled under the bars. Its head was mostly covered with beak, no eyes, only a few stubby protrusions near the top like crusty feathers. Standing in the crimson path, its nether end seemed to drink as if through its claws, and a misty patch above its head appeared, in which there was a hazy outline and the suggestion of a voice.

"Report."

"No sign. The men are in position. If they don't come by the coast road, they'll never make Cryssigens before the ides. We'll be ready for them."

"Three days, at most," the voice commanded, "delay them where you are in the hills and even the fastest horse could never make Cryssigens before the conference."

"We'll do what we can," Skeer said doubtfully, "it depends how many men they bring, what arms—"

"It does not," the voice was still sexless but cracked like a whip, "you will expend every drop of blood if need be, everything we supplied, make sure no one survives to pass you. Rout or death, those are the only options you will hold open to the Emperor's men."

"But, they may bear the flag! Survivors will talk—and the creature," Skeer protested, "it is still half-trained."

"Every asset. You can die in the attempt and still be safe from me."

The peasant had stopped moaning and gurgling through the rag, and the flow of blood slowed; now the vision began to fade. Skeer planted his foot on the stomach and pushed hard, causing one more rush of red to keep the contact.

"I understand!" he snapped.

"By dawn on the thirteenth, your work will have succeeded. Spare nothing until then."

The misty shape faded away. The minor demon in the cage immediately stepped back from the cooling, stilled blood and hunkered down to stare blindly in his direction. Skeer regarded the horrid thing with distaste. Its one snake-like stinging tendril he had severed leaving the shorter claw arm, which could not harm him through the bars. But everything about it, from the unearthly color of its hide, to its bizarre rustling inside the cage, to the way it seemed to sense when their mutual master was about to use it for the mind-talk spell; all spoke to the world beyond that men like Skeer had no desire to think about.

He strode forth from the cave, scanning the encampment of his bandit-tribe, the few peasant trulls left alive to cook and clean and serve desire, and the surrounding hills and valleys of the border range. The voice was correct—tomorrow marked the Tenth of the Dolphin, and a fast horseman with post-changes could hardly hope to make Cryssigens in less than two full days. So even if the Emperor's mission arrived—the master's agent in the city assured it left a few days ago—he had only to delay them here three days. Of course, Skeer reflected, any survivors meant tales told of men who defied the Emperor's authority. Could he hope to destroy them to the last man? Worth a few of his own to try. And if not—as lucrative as tolls on the coast road had been, it might be prudent to withdraw to the Gelvorging Deep for the summer.

Of course, he could not bring everything with him. That hell-thing in the cave, he would gladly abandon, as well as some vagrants among his crew. He surveyed the barricades of his hilltop covert, the stacks of brush for flame-traps and the black-drenched arrows piled up for the coming battle. As he thought about the need for food during the withdrawal, the entire camp was again buffeted by the harsh, ear-splitting echoes of the monster raging against its confinement. The peasants and a few of his men fell to the ground, and everyone froze, some clutching uselessly at their skulls to protect against the searing blast of noise from the walled-off enclosure in the back of the camp. Men's screams mingled with its echoes, and Skeer checked his long-handled crop with its green gem inset as if it could defend him.

At that moment, had someone claimed Skeer was afraid, he would not have laughed. But the enclosure's tree trunk bars held and the handler forked another slab of meat through the access hole. Behind him, his men dragged out the bloody corpse and stacked it in the trash-midden, where refuse and broken things of all types lay tangled. The captured peasants moaned at the familiar sight, and one murmured to another, "What does he hope to gain by torturing us? What does he want to know?"

Skeer looked at the midden speculatively. Not all food had to walk on four legs, during a march such as this. Then again, best not to get it too used to certain tastes. But first, he must stop the Emperor's mission.

The peasantry of the Mark believed Skeer Two-Eye a bandit, preying on trade and the locals due to the ignorance of the powers, not with their support. Best not to let them think too much on his unusual arrangement. With a small sign, Skeer indicated to the men the whisperer would be next. Tomorrow night the master would need another report.

*J*ustin marched the dekents until moonset, long enough to get beyond the city precinct and out into the rural Domain. Then he called a halt until sunrise. He could have forced them much longer without sleep; all but one in his command were elves, and he knew Tass would die before admitting his inability. But just because unwounded elves could do without sleep didn't mean they were better soldiers for it. Rest was needed to relieve the fatigue of the march, and he wanted to drill them in making camp, good practice for less friendly lands ahead.

M'nesa saw to his men and the horses according to the manual, and was already rotating chores evenly, taking his turn with the others. Tass, who put the foot dekent to one side, had a different approach. First taking the toughest chore on himself, he announced each task as a surprise, clearly going in order of whichever of them had annoyed him the most. He evolved pet-names for each soldier to go with his best wishes; the first elf to protest his assignment was dubbed Kiss-up, and bore that name with welted ribs on his way to gather brush. The older recruits, looking ten years beyond Tass and perhaps two or three times his age for all he knew, he lovingly referred to as Lad and Lass. Justin made a private bet as to who would dig and bury the latrine, and won; Kein Trador was known only as "Strategos" to his human officer, and took the spade without a word.

Lying under the stars Justin contemplated the difficulty before him. Assuming Valin did his job, and stayed ignorant of his part in the larger scheme, their best hope would be to enter the city by another way, so as to sever the connection with the direct south. After crossing the border into the barony of Cesmir, they should swing northeast into Gaden along the Earthcut River. Justin had heard the farmers of the center-lands were less overtly hostile to the emperor than the cities and coast. The memory of raids from the desert was always fresh there, and imperial force had sometimes been required to keep them in check. In recent years, it was true, there had been little trouble. But if Justin could talk to some local knights or merchants, while pretending to look for work, he might get a better sense of the politics taking place in Cryssigens. Then to enter from the east, perhaps five or six days after Valin won the delay, he would still have eight or nine weeks to find a solution. No doubt Hansen would want to hear from him before then; but Justin doubted he would make anyone completely happy on this mission. First get some news, then find the contact who could help send the message. He regarded the ax-scribed ring and wondered what approach he could use to sift out a good ruler from among the emperor's enemies. But neither ring nor stars volunteered an answer.

Rising with the sun, the unit cleared camp—"The strategos will sweep the trash into the latrine and bury it", Tass announced—and set out on their first serious day of marching. Overnight hikes had been a standard feature of the training course, and Justin reckoned that only tonight would he have a true sense of the unit's morale. Second night on hard ground without tents, after ten hours of marching would sift out the complaints for him to deal with, hopefully once and for all. And he intended to set a good pace.

Marching speed, as the manual pointed out, was a question of morale in the end. Men could be double-timed or force marched on orders without testing their willingness. But in a very short while, the body slows unless inspired; this was not disloyalty but a lack of focus, and even the training had not stretched their limits as a real campaign would. Justin hoped to avoid any fighting, but he had to know what he dealt with here. These were his men; he couldn't ask of them until he knew what they could give. Marching, above all, was boring work.

"We will march at double-speed for an hour, then normal pace for an hour, until I am satisfied," Justin announced crisply from horseback. He set out at the head of the column without hesitation, and the men fell in step behind. M'nesa's horsemen matched their pace to that of the foot dek for the first hour. As the infantry slowed for the second hour, M'nesa ordered the cavalry to dismount; they marched alongside the foot soldiers for that time, good sense to rest the mounts though some of the riders took it a little ill.

"The manual calls for a quarter-hour's walk and three-quarters of riding," one sulked to a compatriot. Justin had no time to wonder if he should speak, for M'nesa said agreeably, "Yes, for unified force, but not combined arms units, about which the manual is still silent. We shall make sure that our own legs can match those of the horses."

Tass, overhearing this scowled a bit and said, "No doubt, we shouldn't tax the horse-boys too much, gentlemen." There was some grinning back and forth between the lines over this. M'nesa thought awhile and said, "My fellow dek is quite correct—Captain, we should like at the next rotation to march during the double-time hour."

The cavalry cried aloud at this, while the infantry called out praises. Tass, cresting the group, barked, "Let us not wait to accommodate our brethren, but go at double-time now then!"

"What! You expect us to make double-time for two hours in a row?"

"Demon sweat, no! Not without singing, you don't!" Tass rejoined, "Let me hear 'The World's Turned Upside-Down' there, Minstrel," Tass said awarding another nickname. "Nice and loud, so's we can all hit the chorus together."

Justin nodded that the double-time should restart, and Tass kept a beat with his hand slapping the shield to get them up to speed. "Sing, Minstrel!" he roared, and the soldier lurched into the drinking-song that had taken over the land these past several months. As "Minstrel" started the line, the soldiers all gave the responses with mouth and hand.

> *It seems to me our luck's run out*
> *WHAT ELSE, WE'RE SOLDIERS NOW*
> *If the job's too hard, it's ours no doubt*
> *Clap-Clap! BUT NEVER QUESTION HOW*

The song was a parody of the lay some fawning bard had written to commemorate Yula's defeat of Viridian's evil dynasty the previous summer. The sentiment of the original, entitled "The Demons are Put Down" rang hollow with a nation shocked to discover the treachery that had captured its throne. A much-less complimentary version— touting the dwarf's shortness, his murderous temper, his lack of noble class, and any number of imagined failings—became an overnight success. With the same tune and a different chorus, it was sung with varying degrees of gusto across the empire—now called "The World's Turned Upside-Down". The imperial soldiers, even during training, had hammered out their own flavorings, with endless verses for every situation.

> *Well we had it good in the demon's day*
> *But Yula had to have his say*
> *And since the battle of Tor Perite*
> THE WORLD'S TURNED UPSIDE-DOWN

The men ground out the second hour at double-time, and Justin called a brief halt. Sweating and blown, yet the men were hardening into something now, and the rivalry between horseman and infantry was helping the dekentars gain some respect as well. Justin pushed ahead with the third hour, still at double-time, and the horsemen this time needed no urging to stay afoot. There would be some blisters tomorrow, Justin realized, but without delay he dismounted as well and walked with them. The reaction of the men to this sight was tangible.

During the afternoon, M'nesa took his cavalry away from the road to maneuver, exercising the horses and still catching up easily to the rest before their riding-hour was up. Every double-time hour, Tass ordered the men to sing, picking out the leaders with his usual perverse sense of who would like it least. And he took a turn himself, his powerful voice hitting perhaps three of the song's six notes, and none in the correct places.

> *We fight more than we breathe I swear*
> WHAT ELSE, WE'RE SOLDIERS NOW
> *Go give the North Mark knights a scare*
> *Clap-Clap!* BUT NEVER QUESTION HOW
> *Break their ranks with your brains alone*
> *Never mind how many fall and moan*
> *Now there's a dwarf upon the throne*
> AND THE WORLD'S TURNED UPSIDE-DOWN

"Dekentar Tass," one man cried, "we'll force-march the rest of the hour, only please don't sing anymore." A roar of laughter greeted this, and Tass along with them. Justin signaled for them both to approach at the head of the line as they marched.

"Tass, what do you know about the land ahead? We'll be clear of the Domain in two days."

"Precious little, captain," Tass admitted with one wrist raised to show the manacle-marks. "furloughs were even more difficult to get in my previous job."

"The city then, what can we expect of Cryssigens?"

"Ah, the city," the human responded and sighed with something like longing. "Captain, Argens is the largest city in the Lands of Hope, they say—"

"In the northern kingdoms," M'nesa cut in, "they say Conar the City of Wonders is twice the size."

"It's a lie!" Tass rejoined without malice, "But size isn't everything … in cities, of course," that last in a raised voice for the men to chuckle at. "Now Cryssigens—not a tenth as big as Argens, sir, but everything there is so rich and fine. Day-laborers wear bright red and blue, and anyone with any uppity-ness to them wears silk. Wine's more common than water, the kids drink it from age three," Tass nodded around to the marching men who were clearly listening in and expressing surprise. "Nobles pass by, like in Argens, takes an hour with all the train, and every day's another celebration of something. To the chapel this day, the arena next, then the theater; being a noble in Cryssigens, it's exhausting work, not like this little pleasure-hike!"

"Where do you go for information? The latest news and rumors?"

Tass eyed Justin a bit thoughtfully. "Well the taverns, if you don't care whether the news is true or not."

"Of course, for accurate news!" Justin exclaimed in exasperation.

"Oh, not for entertainment then," Tass said without taking insult. "If you want the best gossip, you must to temple."

"To temple?"

"Aye, the Stargazers, all the connected folks go to their parties. Or to services—it's beyond a poor man like me to tell the difference." Swinging around to march backwards, Tass addressed the entire unit.

"The priestesses of Argens Stargazer are without doubt the most juicy women in the world, men. Nobles in Cryssigens pay their thousand silver—"

"Thousand!" several men cried at once.

"I said a thousand! And not to see whomever they wish—not the way it works. They pay to have their name inscribed on a list. And then, after waiting so long their manhood is like to crumble away, they get the word they can attend that very evening. And the man is always free—no refunds."

"Attend what?" even M'nesa was becoming interested. Tass put on a knowing look and said, "A private session."

As he spoke, Tass lengthened his backward-stride, and the men started increasing pace to keep in earshot. "Private?" one asked, "with a priestess?" The Stargazer sect was the most wealthy, and mysterious of the various cults of Argens. Its leaders were versed in astrology and forecasting the future, much prized by merchants and political leaders alike. And the sect emphasized Argens' legendary prowess as a progenitor. The Stargazers countenanced multiple spouses, for either the man or woman who could master the art of loving and supporting more than one mate. The comparison to whores seemed obvious, though to Justin's limited understanding Stargazers turned out to be just as constant and monogamous as others. But they were definitely less ashamed of liaisons and frank talk.

"How do you know all this?" Justin quietly challenged his subaltern.

"I got a silver token, myself," Tass proudly alleged and it was some minutes before he could shout down the objections from all sides. By now he was backpedaling at a trot, and the men were marching beyond double-time though it was not the hour. "It was for winning in the arena—I made some powerful men a lot of money, I understand, so they wanted to reward me."

"Are there gold and silversteel tokens as well," M'nesa asked as if for scholarly purposes, and Tass nodded but made a face.

"Sure, if all you want to do is talk. The higher ranked priestesses all make themselves available. Silver and a lovely acolyte is fine with me. Oh, my, was it fine…"

Justin stared at nothing as he thought. The legend of the Stargazers formed an aspect of this he had not anticipated, but it might prove less unpleasant than his average duty. And it made sense that the temple would be an excellent vantage point from which to gain the news. If one could keep focus … he realized the men were leering at him, and got back on his horse to mask his embarrassment.

Past noon the next day, while exercising Furta with M'nesa's dek, Justin was the first to notice men on the road ahead. He signaled the assembly and the two lines rejoined in good time.

"Soldiers," several voices called out, and Tass added, "Aye, all the same height."

It was indeed the foot-dekents of Valin's company, marching north with unremarkable pace and shoddy formation towards the distant hills that marked the border of the Imperial Domain and the North Mark. No other horsemen in sight—Valin had left his infantry at least four hours' march behind, for how long only Argens knew. Justin felt his jaw tighten and he spurred Furta forward to speak with them alone.

At the sound of his horse approaching, the lines moved to the right side, but continued ahead; neither dekentar saluted as a captain reined in. The men all kept their view straight ahead, which was correct by the book but hardly normal.

"Has your captain ordered a rear-guard action?"

"No. Captain. We are marching as ordered."

"How far ahead is the main body?" The dekentar who spoke first screwed up his face and hesitated before answering.

"I … don't know. We saw them yesterday midafternoon—"

"You have been out of contact overnight!" Justin's voice thundered with outrage, and the subalterns both flinched. If anything, their marching pace had slowed even more since he had seen them. "Did you make camp then, and was that with or without orders?"

"We—we stopped when it got full dark. Figured it was best to march fresh, not knowing…" the elf's voice trailed off in misery, and Justin realized he had no orders at all. He might have done the same as this dekentar, himself—but the fog of war was supposed to be created by the enemy, not your own commanding officer.

Justin's dekents were now approaching up the road, even at their normal pace overtaking the group. The manual was right—these deks were no worse trained, their men no weaker than the ones Tass had chosen. Maybe better, on the surface. But they were acting like defeated men, before any taste of combat. Even veterans in their ranks, such as the two dekentars, caught the sickness of low morale. Justin stopped his interrogation, partly because his men were now within earshot and partly because it was time for deeds, not words.

Striding up to the head of Valin's foot-column, Justin's men continued with their easy banter. Unconsciously, the others picked up their pace a shade and marched more closely in step. Tass, without seeming to notice or care, quickened his shield-tap just a bit, until they were exceeding normal march speed. Justin reckoned they had sliced almost a half-day off the total march since leaving Argens already, what with the competition.

M'nesa pretended to consult the sun and ordered the dismount, though it was not yet the hour. Some of Valin's men, misinterpreting the gesture, stopped and began to unlimber their gear. But M'nesa looked up to Justin and said innocently, "Time for the double-speed hour, sir?" And the captain nodded, sensing the mood.

At once Tass began to beat the double-time, and Justin's men moved off so quickly that Valin's deks were left in disarray. Scrambling to catch up, they were a few rods back by the time they got in order. But glancing south, Justin could see some determination in their eyes. Damned to hell if they were going to let a flagless mercenary beat them to the border of the North Mark.

"Sing, Strategos!" Tass bellowed, and Trador from the back of the line was a little shocked. After a few beats, he complied with a smile:

> *Oh Tass will lead us straight to hell*
> *WHAT ELSE, WE'RE SOLDIERS NOW*
> *And it won't be long, we all can tell*
> *Clap-Clap! BUT NEVER QUESTION HOw*
> *Can we wait him out, now there's a thought*
> *A few years left is all he's got*
> *Take orders from a man-why not?*
> *WHEN THE WORLD'S TURNED UPSIDE-DOWN*

Tass turned to grin beatifically at Trador, a checker-toothed promise of misery that evening, but the men all roared for an encore. By the second time, even Valin's men were singing the chorus.

When they bivouacked that night, Justin gave a few orders to Valin's deks about dispositions and they accepted without question. And with salutes. Informally and for the moment, the size of his command had doubled: at this pace, by the time he got to Cryssigens he could take the city by storm. On a turn around the camp during the early watch, he spoke to Valin's men, neutrally and without prying, and learned much he already suspected. Valin had set the pace to the mounted deks right from the start, gradually leaving his infantry behind as if they annoyed him. They had caught up to camp the first night, and were assigned the remaining watches while the horsemen slept.

It was beyond credit, but Justin knew this was just the way Valin would act. Lying back beneath the brilliant stars, he cursed under his breath. Why not take ten cavalry deks, if all he wanted was speed? Of course, because the manual suggested at least one to five in infantry at the pentadek level and higher. Justin thought closer to four-to-six was probably best—too many situations where cavalry could not be used to full effect. But Valin, he knew, would have none of that. He had been too unsure, and could not defy the manual—but he was too impatient to truly lead the men he had recruited. They could be Justin's for the taking now, he knew it.

But that was all wrong. He couldn't march into Cryssigens at the head of forty men and pretend he was impoverished. He hadn't drawn enough money to supply them, for one thing. His secret mission would be seriously impaired if he didn't get these infantry back to their commander. Once through the border hills and to the bridge by the Earthcut, he could part ways and wish the poor bastards well. But was that even feasible? Justin tried to calculate. No—horsemen moving at cavalry pace would already be well beyond the foothills now. He had to admit, Valin's schedule would have been tight if he'd waited too long for his infantry. But by leaving them behind, he'd ensured they would march at a snail's pace—there was probably no way to bring the command back together now. These men were his responsibility.

Argens strike the bastard —but then as the silence of night settled down Justin had a strange thought. Valin was no bastard in the eyes of the law, of course. He was a loyal son—he could easily have stayed at home and inherited the foef. Why, Justin wondered for the first time, did he leave rank and comfort to enlist in the officer's corps at all? Ambition? But he was already a knight, and could have commanded nearly as many men in his foef's retainers as he did now. Was he impoverished? Possibly—Justin's father had precious little when he last armed for war. Even ten years of an officer's pay, in a time of peace, wouldn't amount to a single good season's tithing on lands as well placed as Valin's. The more he thought, the less he felt he knew his rival: during the training, Justin had tried to give him as little notice as he could. Admittedly, he had half-believed Valin was there only to cause him pain. Yet nothing could have been more ridiculous, that was just his own wretched self-pity talking.

He deliberated dismissing the men back to Argens, but decided it wouldn't work. Despite his rank, the men knew that Justin was a wash-out, a "bought badge" with no authority to order soldiers who marched under the Emperor's banner. It would invite disobedience, and maybe even a fight. He could see nothing better than to bring them along. But damn Valin T'lenthor to the deepest hottest hell for this. Again, he wondered why but to no effect. Only when Justin decided that he could decide nothing about Valin, did he drop off to a few hours' sleep.

$$\oplus \oplus \oplus$$

Justin dreamed that the answer to Valin and the extra men lay somewhere in the manual; but he kept searching his old quarters back in the compound and couldn't find it. He woke with dry mouth and a feeling of dismay that would not dissipate as the company ate and started marching. The more he thought, the less he liked his chances, as they left the smooth flat lowland of the Imperial Domain and marched up into the hill-country bordering on the North Mark.

But Justin's mind cleared marvelously, once they came to the village where people were dying.

The troops had passed through any number of these hamlets on the march, and compared to the sight and smell of road dust they were interesting enough. This one seemed particularly small—little more than a gather of cottages nestled in a large dell—and sleepy even though it was mid-morning. The first signal of human habitation was an older woman's scream. As the men snapped to alert, she hobbled in sight along the road. Seeing the soldiers she cried incoherently and held out an arm. Around the cottage corner an axe came hurtling, and she fell with her neck half-severed. The sounds of men fighting and shouting became more audible.

Justin snapped Furta around to face the men. "Tass, take your dek down the main street. Secure against all combat—men with weapons are enemies. Flush them out to us on the other side. Zetee, your men with me." Lashing lightly on the mare's flanks, Justin led the cavalry in a loop around the west side of the houses. Tass pointed to all the infantry, and without hesitation thirty men followed him into the village.

The move worked to perfection. Even as he rode, Justin could hear the confused outrage of the attackers, and Tass' bull voice calling out orders and cursing with his joyous gusto. The cavalry, with spears couched high, came around to the north side road. There they saw a spill of armed men routing right into their laps. Against eleven trained cavalry with lances, they fell like cut wheat in a windstorm. Justin hacked down two routers with his sword, the second with his flat because he wanted a prisoner. In just moments, the action had gone from a lopsided fight to mere herding of captives; eight of the original score or so survived, whereas two of the infantry had sustained walking wounds.

The villagers had not been so fortunate—as Justin saw them creep forth and tend to the bodies everywhere, it seemed to him that two in three had been slain. This brazen attack, so close to the Imperial Domain, looked far worse than anything he had envisioned. Who in the North Mark allowed such lawlessness? And where was Valin?

Dismounting, Justin approached the surviving villagers to learn what he could, while M'nesa minded the prisoners in a sheep-pen and Tass oversaw the gathering of bodies for funeral.

"They came from the hills this morning, Captain. We've had some raids these past few months, sure. And no one goes the north road without a guard. But we've never seen a bandit within reach of the town before."

"From the hills, you say. Are there many of them?"

Shrugs, shakes of head, muttered avoidances. No one knew, but the general idea was that there were many, and getting more so. One man spoke up, "I've heard tell, sir, that their leader is Skeer Two-Eye, that vandal who used to haunt the Gelvorging forest further north. He's always taken tolls in the deep woods there, but the traffic is more frequent here."

"Where in the hills? Nearby?" No one knew.

"Where is the cavalry that came ahead of us?"

"That was last night, sir. Spent the evening here outside town, and moved on at first light." Gone more than six hours, then: Justin felt his stomach start to knot up as he searched the road north into the hills. Time for the prisoners.

By the sheep pen M'nesa stood with several of his riders, watering their mounts and exchanging easy jests. He looked for all the world as if he still awaited a call to action instead of having routed robbers and saved a village. Tass, finished with burial dispositions and seeing the cremation fires started, sauntered over while drawing something from his belt. The human fell in beside Justin and M'nesa as they entered the pen with the eight human wolves.

They stood ranged about, most hugging some wound or other. Stripped of their weapons they looked more than naked. Fear clutched them now, and Justin sensed as he scanned their faces that fear had driven them most of their lives. This morning's raid was probably the first time they could feel in charge of anything … and instead, they'd run into Emperor's men. He almost felt pity, until the crackle of the fires reminded him. One man stood out to Justin's eye; his training as a noble elf picked up on the way the others were facing, and his stance just a half-step closer. Surely, he'd led this rabble.

"You there, answer on your life. Where have you come from, and who told you to raid this village?"

"We live in the hills. No one told us, we just…" The vandal-elf couldn't hold Justin's gaze for long.

"Your leader is a bandit named Skeer." Justin accused, and the man started to nod, then shrugged. "No doubt he's had a fat time of things recently," Justin taunted, "but he's tasted the wrong end of a lance by now."

The man's head snapped up with a spark, "Them! We've already fixed them up proper, which is when the lads and me, we…" too late, he sensed the trap and shut his jaw with an audible click. So—their discipline was nothing to boast of. Justin took a step nearer, casually, and the man stepped back, less so.

"What has happened to the cavalry that entered these hills this morning?"

The elf tried to give back fire in his eyes; it guttered in Justin's face but he said nothing. Tass stepped past him, saying, "Captain, if you'll allow me?"

The item from his belt was a kind of glove, and Tass donned it now on his shield-hand. A thick leather gauntlet with overlapping metal plates on the knuckle side, each studded plate snapped into place as he flexed his fist. Smiling, Tass stepped up to the luckless prisoner with both thumbs hooked in his belt, saying in a friendly tone "I guess you didn't hear the Captain. He wants to know what happened to the horsemen from this morning."

He stood sideways to the prisoner and leaned slightly towards him as if straining to hear. After two counts, Tass' left hand snapped out with a jab to the bandit's jaw. Before the bandit hit the mud, Tass's hand was back in its belt as if he hadn't moved. The villain lolled in the dirt with blood from his jaw and cheek streaming around his hand. The other prisoners had not moved a muscle throughout, and none stirred to hinder Tass or help their fellow.

"Can you hear any better now? Should I repeat the question?"

The elf struggled to speak, spat out some blood and cursed, "I won't talk, Skeer'd kill me in an instant if he knew."

"Ah," Tass rejoined gladly, "but the thing about a cestus is, I can hit you with it all day, and you might not die." With his right hand alone, Tass seized the elf's collar and hauled him to his knees. "Now then, what's it to be?" And here he gently rubbed the back of his cestus on the man's shoulder, wiping off a little skin as if giving it back.

Less than ten minutes later, the men were marching double-time out of the village north along the road. Justin had detailed one dekent of Valin's men to march the prisoners back to Argens with a message for Commander Hansen's eyes only. The rest were in battle formation, the cavalry ranging to either side of the road where the ground was most open, and the two infantry dekents in column ahead, shields out and spears ready. The bandits confessed that Valin's men had been ambushed; no clear picture of how many casualties, but they were stopped cold in the border hills a few hours' march away.

Riding at the column head Justin felt more apprehension as the hills steepened, the road became more winding, and the trees hunched in ever closer. He could not have designed terrain more suited to an ambush if he were making one of those battle-scenes in a box they used back at the academy. He could picture his men as the miniature figures they used, and his imagination peppered the forest with bandits, shifting around his flanks, closing off his retreat. From deep within he felt an urge to ride ahead with the cavalry and establish contact. But his mind ruled; he knew that as Valin's way, and a mistake. He glanced up at the sun, near mid-day on the 11th. Three days at least to Cryssigens from here.

In the face of the tension his instinct for command came alive. "M'nesa, send two men in rotation ahead to scout, and have them report back on the half-hour. Tass, two-arms formation." His dekentars nodded and passed the orders on. A pair of men rode off at a canter, while the back half of each infantry dek switched to longbows. The easy chatter died down and the men became watchful. The road rang with the sound of boots, sinfully loud as the rocks and clefts became steeper. The returning rounds of horsemen found nothing and the hours dragged into afternoon. Justin allowed just the briefest pauses, and only Tass had the stomach for jokes. Now the sun was out of sight and shadows cloaked the vales they marched in. The road had petered down to a mere suggestion of packed earth—other spurs and tracks constantly branched from it and keeping the men to pace seemed more and more unwise. The echoes of their boots and hooves gave them away for a league.

Another pair of horsemen returned with nothing to report, and M'nesa called off the rotation. He turned to Justin and said "They've been around us for at least an hour, some. They're waiting their time."

Justin had spotted movement as well, probably not deer or cats, and nodded in agreement. "We can hope it's because we outnumber them." M'nesa smiled politely and rejoined, "If we do, then so did Valin."

Two hours later everyone was on edge when the sounds of men ahead materialized. The road north twisted around an enormous shelf of rock on the left, with trees hemming the right side to within arm's reach. The view was completely blocked, though small flares of light showed at intervals. It was nearly dark as night, but elven vision still accounted well outdoors. Justin throttled the instinct to rush ahead and turned again to his officers. "Tass, send a dek to take that rock from this side. M'nesa, horsemen to the rear." This perceived demotion sent a loud ripple through the cavalry, which M'nesa ignored. Tass sent Valin's dek up the rock and Justin's original troops double-timed around the bend.

Twenty rods ahead the draw was bottle-necked on both sides by rocky slopes stippled with stubborn small evergreens. Armed men, bearing the Emperor's uniform, stood with interlocked shields along two sides of a defensive square: the rock wall, two supply wagons and a large pine formed cover to the other two sides. Most of Valin's men were on foot and dead horses lay everywhere. Small fires around the draw broke the darkness in many places, and more streaks of flame rained down in lazy arcs from the steeps on both sides. Beyond, where the road narrowed to a pass lay a massive pile of brush and logs, blocking the way and still smoldering.

"Forward! Hold your return fire until ordered." With a shout of "aye" the men surged ahead, and the square opened to receive them. Justin estimated at least sixty men still upright, but hardly enough horses to mount them. The bandits occupied the heights on three sides and were sending down fire-arrows; probably aimed at the horses first. Two of the wagon-train mounts sagged dead in their traces, most of the surviving horses sheltered under the pine and against the rock to keep them out of arrow's path.

Before Justin could call out to ask, he saw Valin lying among a hedgerow of the wounded in the lee of the rock. As he dismounted and ran to his rival's side, Justin saw an arrow sticking from his chest, and other wounds including burns on both his arms. In one hand he clutched the broken hilt of his sword, in the other the blood-stained flag of mission, as if his fingers could not let go. He half-stifled a gargle of pain and struggled to focus on this newcomer through a haze that misted his clear green eyes.

"Justin!" he barked, "Hah! What a welcome sight for you, here to witness my undeserved fate. What mischievous chance brings the sight of you."

"Valin, why are you lingering here, fool? You needed your infantry, you must regroup!"

"Demons take delay! You lecture me? What could you know of my mission, you failed bought-badge?" He coughed hard enough to rip his attempted oath in half. "We had to win through, but the bastards blocked the road. There's no time!"

"You need foot soldiers to clear the way!" Justin was beside himself with frustration. All these good men wasted. And horses too; looking over to the barricade north, Justin made out the ruined corpse of Sirocco, impaled on the spike-limbs the bandits had carved. All Justin's anger and tension boiled over then; turning back he seized Valin by the front of his mail shirt and pulled him up close. "You charged a barricade unsupported!"

"Seven times," Valin croaked, and ripped another groan of pain that forced its way past Justin's hatred. He now saw Valin's body had three more arrows in it, with the shafts broken off. The arrow-tips were daubed in something black, and his smoking wounds were streaked with it, coloring the edges and spreading under his skin. He could feel heat from Valin's body, and eased him back to the earth as the man's eyes swarmed in all directions.

A fire arrow sizzled into the ground not four feet from them, and Justin saw half of Valin's face by its glare as he bit down against the pain. "Such a loss for the empire," Valin hissed through gritted teeth, "its greatest officer on his first mission". He already knew he was dying. Justin looked down on him with cooling fury, yet could not restrain himself completely. "The empire has lost more of value," he growled, "in that horse."

Valin did not hear as he convulsed on the ground. By the light of the fires Justin could see dark tinges spreading in the veins under his skin, through his arms, up his neck, around his skull. Holding his breath like a man who knew the number left, Valin grasped Justin's arm and pulled him down. Slapping the pole of the mission flag into Justin's palm he let out a shout, yelling, "Orders now—reach Cryssigens—before Ides—"

"No," Justin choked, shaking his head, "No, no, you must—" He tried to let go of the flag, but Valin's death-clench was becoming literal.

"Shut up! Thyme, your disgrace—poor performance ... doesn't matter. The Empire! Mission—more important. Delay the vote—then wait—Hansen's orders—" Valin drew one more ragged breath, but never let it out, freezing instead with eyes and mouth open, body clenched and the small of his back off the earth.

"Orders!" Justin bellowed at Valin as if he could still hear. "From myself!" In his hand he could feel the flagpole touching his ring as a shock of realization coursed through him. Planting it solidly at Valin's feet, Justin doffed his riding cape and put it over his rival's face. He stood and regarded the flag as a captured man looks at the gallows. Beyond the golden sun symbol at the center, and the red blotches on its edge, he saw ranged about him more than four-score fighting men. He heard the sound of the wounded, the cough of frightened horses, the lick of flames. Down from the night sky, sharp-pointed stars of doom kept falling, to stick and hiss in earth or wood, or flesh.

The knight and hardened warrior he had been might have looked for help. But the captain Justin had become rose within him as before. He seized the flag of mission—again the click against his ring—and carried it to Furta, posting it in the saddle-socket before mounting up. He wheeled to face the men.

"I assume command." A simple statement, backed by all his training and made to sound as if he'd ordered the moons to rise. "Dekentars, to me." Three men shuffled forward to join Tass and M'nesa; so few, but one more stood on the rise behind them. And a man signaled from among the wounded, "I can stand, captain, I just cannot walk—it's broken, sir."

"Oversee the injured then, make sure all arrow wounds are thoroughly washed; use the moss, if we have any to draw out that tar. You," to one of the new dekentars, "find extra spear points, make some hook-and-ropes. We're going to pull down that barricade." He raised his voice to all the men. "The wounded ride in the wagons, get rid of everything that would take a space from a living man. Use any horse to pull them, we'll sort out who is cavalry later. On the rocks, there! Fire wherever you see torchlight and provide some cover."

"You three—unlimber that wagon team and follow me. Tass and M'nesa, move out on my order."

"Captain! So few?" "We've been trying all day!"

"I need men I can trust," Justin returned shortly, and as he felt their shock he could tell the barb was set. To Valin's men he called out, "Every able man of you, keep in readiness—and on foot. We're saving the horses."

Men formed up with a sense of purpose now, grumbling but armed and ready to open the square. Justin gave M'nesa the "hold" hand-signal, then leaned down to his human subaltern, pitching his voice so all could hear.

"Tass," he said without hesitation, "take me that barricade."

The human's grin was aft of his ears. He roared a command to his dek as they barged out through the opened space. Justin urged his horse to a trot next to the wagon-team, keeping his shield high and on the lookout for fire-arrows. All about the gorge the energy began changing. The men on the rocks scored two hits from their improved vantage, and the troops shouted encouragement to each other. The enemy seemed to realize their problem, now that their foe was watching from the rocks; very few fire-arrows flew any more.

But the barricade was imposing, and Justin could see several forms lurking on the rocks near each end as well as behind the tangle of brush and fallen trunks. Three pines lay over each other, with the largest branches stripped and sharpened to act as spikes; brush bundles without number wedged between them made close approach difficult. Indecision here would cost lives, but of course Tass had none. Leaping partway up the left-hand rock, he wielded his thrusting spear above the shoulder; dodging an axe overhead and taking a large rock on his shield, he laughed and gauged where the enemy stood. Right at the top, two bandits crouched near a pine and reached for more rocks to throw down. Tass hurled his spear, not made for the job, with such strength it completely impaled one of the men against the tree. He had plenty of time, before he expired, to look to his companion, who simply fell down the backside in fear. Surmounting the rock, Tass wrenched the spear free and kicked off the corpse, yelling to his troop, "I know you can live forever, but will you ever be MEN!" His dek had long ago had enough of this: on the other side, Kein Trador vaulted to the summit using the branch bundles as springs and engaged three men at once. The rest of the dek swarmed behind them on both sides and down again, into the swirling shapes beyond.

Justin used this ample time to get the wagon-team turned with the help of the drovers. He whirled the grapple-ropes and caught them both solidly on trunks, then lashed the team back up the draw. With four horses pulling hard, the tangled clot of timber shivered, creaked, snapped loose and came away. Tass's men were already hammering the bandits on the other side, armor and training holding their own against numbers. Justin signaled to M'nesa and the sound of horses' hooves, as much as their plight, did the enemy in. They gave way at once, losing the narrow pass, and Justin plunged in with his sword ahead of the charge.

Even as he stabbed and wheeled, Justin kept his eye on the heights to both sides. "Come on," he muttered, "so few of us. We're new, we could be routed … come on, bite at it." His men were outnumbered two to one even after the initial shock of M'nesa's cavalry. It only seemed an hour before he made out shapes through the darkness. Scores of the bandits creeping to the edge of the fighting; an unlit arrow snapped into his head and glanced off the hawk-helmet. Justin was surprised but had the presence of mind to slump to the side as if the bolt had penetrated.

The ruse worked; with a ragged yell, the sides of the draw boiled alive with bandits firing last shots and wielding short blades or miscellaneous weapons. Now, time to see if Justin had gambled away their lives, or whether Valin's men had found a new captain. Justin snapped erect, seized the mission flag and waved it in the attack-signal. "Yula! The Empire!"

"The Empire!" came the cry from back at the camp, and Valin's former cadre shot forth to take the bandits on level ground. Most of the villains did not see enough, or in time. The soldiers, keeping in rough lines even on the run, slammed into the melee like a series of waves. Forced to watch as the troop of a bought-badge did what they could not, they were fired now to exceed the valor of their comrades. Superior armor, longer reach with the thrusting spears, discipline, pent-up anger and even numbers all favored the imperial troops now; bandits fell on every side and less than one in five fled into the hills. Four soldiers had died in the assault, including Lass and Minstrel.

Justin took a turn about looking for survivors as the men cheered. When he signaled for quiet, it was given at once; like it or not, he commanded nearly a centar. His secret order, his true mission was in ruins now: no one from the Mark would confide in the agent of the Emperor. But only getting to the table mattered; it was already late evening on the 11th. If a second sunrise found him in these hills, he failed.

"Your former units remain intact," Justin announced. "Dekentars, if your man is wounded, get him to one of the wagons and see to him. One dekentar to sweep the woods on either side, bring back anything you can find and make sure we are not closely watched. We will be on the march by the time you can see the lower moon; each unit-leader will report to me in turn as we go."

"The supplies, captain?"

"Food, if there is room. Personal effects in each man's pack" and here all of Tass's men jeered. "Tents, poles, tables and all furniture go to the funeral pyres." The men groaned, though most of the lost goods had been Valin's anyway. Most importantly, there was no hesitation as the units went about their business. Sixty-odd corpses of the vandals were burned in a massive pile with their old barricade for fuel. Twenty-seven dead soldiers lay on separate, though crowded biers, with Valin at their head. The men sweeping the hills found several pots of the noxious pitch used on the arrows, now poured among the wood as fuel. Justin, standing with a torch near Valin's body under his cloak, searched for a way to speak praise without lying.

"Valin T'lenthor gave his life for the empire," he began slowly, "and though he stood to inherit a fine foef, which I have seen in all seasons and know to be … one of the finest in the Domain … still, he held this of less account than the dream of an empire returned to Hope. Freedom for all men, justice and fair dealing, honest worship restored: Valin T'lenthor." As one, the men called out a salutation, for the knight and their fallen companions. Justin laid the torch on Valin's pyre, then the others in turn. When it was clear the bodies would burn to ash, thus insuring their souls rose on the smoke to heaven, the corps set out.

One of the goods brought to Justin by the reporting dekentars was a hard leather case of coins, Valin's treasury. Justin's allowance fit into a small pouch. The wealth disbursed to Valin gave the new captain an odd feeling, too little to suffice yet too much not to worry about losing. He quietly assigned it to M'nesa, who reported his dek was intact. "And we have our mounts—though not enough for the rest," he added smoothly. Four went to replace one of the wagon teams, and nearly all of the remounts, not shielded by a rider, fell in the early fighting.

"I'll let Tass recruit up to strength tomorrow, Justin said, "If he sees any he likes. Then I'll reform down to the dekentars we have with the others. How many are wounded?"

"Eleven, sir" M'nesa responded. "Most should fight again—but that officer tending them…"

"What of him?"

"Solid man, sir. Yet I doubt he'll be of use in this campaign: weeks for a broken leg, even if it heals properly."

"So then," Justin mused, as if he didn't know. "Two foot dekents, ably led. And of the cavalry … just four." He looked to Zetee with a face of stone. "Are we short one dekentar?"

M'nesa's eyes went wide with surprise, "Are we, sir?"

"Kindly send me Tass. I have some bad news for him." M'nesa saluted with fervor and rode back up the line.

⊕ ⊕ ⊕

*J*ustin called a halt in the hour before dawn and let the men rest until mid-morning of the 12th. He consulted with the dekentars, learned the feel of his new command, and arranged several matters to his liking. But his inner voice kept prompting him to continue at once; now that he held the flag he must forget the ring awhile if not forever. Getting to the city in time was his first charge; finding a new Overlord to support meant nothing without that. Justin could almost see the map in Hansen's office, catching fire and filling his waking vision with smoke. He forced himself to allow four hours' rest only because he expected another attack.

Forenoon they reached halfway through the border hills, winding between mountains on both sides. Justin wished his instincts were less accurate. The scouts ahead reported another barrier, and the company lurched into action. The barricade itself took some time to clear because the enemy set it fully on fire as the company approached; ropes would not work until it died down. But with daylight and morale restored, the fighting effort proved almost perfunctory: less than half an hour saw the bandits in retreat (and not many of them either, Justin noted). His men were starting to feel their oats now, and two dekentars came to him with a formal request to storm the next barrier. Justin nodded, though his heart sank to think they would probably have their chance.

Another hour ahead, another narrow place, and more fallen trees. This time the enemy made a determined effort to resist, and a storm of arrows arced down as the company approached. Tass's dek scoured the hillsides and everyone grinned to hear the rout of the bandit-archers. It took about an hour to clear this log-fire as well, and two of the foot dek carrying the assault died. In late afternoon, mountain shadows fell over the valley; clearly another night would find them in these hills. Why would a mere bandit try to delay them? Justin felt that idea rolling around in his gut and none of the possible explanations gave him any appetite when the men halted to eat.

He scouted the area with his eyes and decided he should pick the battleground. No trees stood in this dell, the hillsides showed lots of bare stone and the way was not narrow enough to block before or behind. Justin ordered a camp, and the men jumped to it.

The company could sense their enemy well before the attack. Elven sight spotted the clumps of bandits working their way down, from only the east side now, staying closer together. Perhaps they believed his company softened up and now tried for the kill, to plunder this hard target. Justin chuckled to realize his position—if he could meet the bandit leader, this Skeer, he would probably offer him every silver piece he had as toll, just to get moving. But no, it felt wrong—Justin had stung them twice already, and the robber could not be that foolish. Then why this form of attack?

The answer came in a hideous, raucous scream that made his men cry out and drop to the earth with hands over ears. Horses panicked; Furta nearly shied out from under Justin, and it took all his skill to maintain his seat. A few moments after the scream, everything shook with the impact of a man-sized stone, which shattered into a thousand lethal fragments tearing through flesh on all sides. Justin looked up to see an enormous winged shape sailing in a curve back to the east. Arrows whistled down among the camp, with the usual indifferent aim but in sufficient number to matter. And they either learned a lesson or ran low on pitch; these missiles weren't lit.

"Hold your positions! Two deks to shelter and corral all horses. Two-arms formation, everyone else. Fire only on dekentar's orders." The men assembled with bowmen behind shield-and-spearmen, scanning the bluffs to the east and waiting. Wounded men groaned where they lay, and at least one man, and three horses, were slain. The occasional arrow thunked into a shield, but the men held their return fire—no small feat with that scream still in their minds.

It returned; another horrible screech of fury and hatred as the shape appeared again far over-head. "Shield-covers, everyone!" Justin bellowed, and the rock hit a little to the left of the camp, showering many with chips and flinders but doing no more damage for the moment. The bandits roared on this signal and rushed into the dell to attack. Justin's bowmen, still taking cover, could not make their volley as effective as otherwise, but bandits fell as they came on. The lightly-armed enemy swarmed into the shield line, but only their numbers gave the soldiers any pause. Reach and discipline took an immediate toll, and the attackers began to fall back. "Follow!" Justin roared, and led the charge on horseback, his only thought to keep close so that the monster might be less useful.

In this he proved wrong again. Though the soldiers did wondrous execution on the retreating enemy, Justin saw the dread shape returning.

His men also saw, and this time began to panic; some fired up hopeless arrows, others went to cover without an order, and every soldier flinched in anticipation. The enemy did not look any happier, and Justin saw betrayal in their eyes as again the scream echoed down. In dismay, he realized his enemy placed no priority on his own men's lives.

The rock scored a direct hit on the melee, crushing a soldier and two bandits together; the shards exploded through men on all sides, cutting them to pieces and spattering gore further than a campfire's heat. Everyone fled in panic, the two sides distinguished only by the direction of the rout. Justin rode after his men, heart swimming with despair. The loss of morale, if it continued, would be fatal. M'nesa ran over, with blood tricking down one shoulder but still a gentle smile on his face.

"I don't quite recall," he ventured, "the section of the manual that deals with this, captain."

Justin had to grin at that—and a moment later Tass, carrying a comrade over his back like a sack of wheat, said "Not to worry, Kiss-up, you'll live to chop our wood tomorrow."

Justin saw horses gathered, wounded men assisted, shields held high on the periphery. Dekentars channeled their shame into shouts and curses, and the men cursed each other for the same reason; but they moved. If his men could do their jobs, so could he.

"Forward! Attack formation with the wagons in the middle. On command, double-time."

Justin calculated he had a few minutes to find cover before the monster returned. The bandits, seeing the shape of things, lost heart and only sent a few arrows his way. Soon, Justin found a spot where the narrow road and thicker trees provided exactly what he had despised an hour ago. He bivouacked the men under cover, and they tipped the wagons sideways to improve matters for the wounded. An hour passed, during which the creature's hideous scream returned two more times, but a clean miss and a harmless closer drop served to settle the men's nerves a bit.

"What is that thing?" one man asked. "Dragon, surely," others responded, though no one among the living had seen a wurm up close.

"Did you notice," Justin asked of the men nearby, "the creature seemed less steady in its flight?" No one had, but he wondered at the long intervals now between its raids. How did a hill-bandit come to control a dragon? It made no sense. But even if the company was safe, the time still ticked away. It was late on the 12th Dolphin. By dawn, a rider needed to be out of these hills, and even then, post-changes or other mishaps might prevent him from reaching Cryssigens by morning on the 15th. By noon of the 13th even a set of Siroccos would not be enough. Justin bitterly reflected that they were pinned here as long as that monster could fly. He could bury the ring and the flag right now.

But he hated moping. Instead Justin walked the small camp, speaking to the men and putting on the appearance of confidence they needed. The men joked with him about their interesting evening, complained about the food (easy enough as they hadn't eaten since breakfast), and sometimes suggested wild schemes to win through. Justin listened to everyone and nodded, checked the wounded, detailed a few men to search for more water. Then he summoned the dekentars, though he had nothing new to say.

"We move at first light. I must gamble that the … that thing up there doesn't want to fly by day so we can make some progress."

The junior officers shifted and looked down, knowing the odds of this.

"There will probably be more barricades. My map isn't that detailed but it would seem the terrain we are in continues another few hours, and they would be foolish not to try again." Nods, silence. It was unfair to test them, but he had to know.

"Or should we retreat, seek reinforcements?" Justin noted with relief how easily the officers passed. All shook their heads, some protested out loud, and one, the oldest with the broken leg, hopped up a pace, and said, "Sir, if you will pardon me. I'm not good for much, few days anyway. You'll be lugging me like firewood, with some of the others … but with both legs and my horse back under me, I must look to the flag for my answer."

Everyone's eye naturally went to the banner, the symbol around which their lives rallied. The veteran pointed and said, "That there is

Captain Valin's blood. And I'd want mine on it too, before we retreat a step. To Cryssigens."

"To Cryssigens," the others avowed together, and M'nesa quietly added, "Hear, hear."

"I am very glad to note your good opinion, and to know that the Empire has such worthy officers. As for tonight's action … men will run, when they don't know what it is they fear. But the fight is not lost until the end, and if they follow the orders we give them, they are soldiers."

He was about to dismiss them, when one of the dekentars cleared his throat.

"Captain? Sir, I was born just north of these hills."

Justin nodded for him to step forward. "Is there another route north to the road?"

"No sir. There are deer-tracks in any direction you could ask, but the pass holds the only road. And I don't … I mean, I haven't been here in many years, sir, so it's likely not worth a thing, but—"

"Out with it."

"They must be on old Bald Top," the dekentar said, looking apologetic and waving his arm to the east. "There's three hundred bandits if there's two, sir-you've seen, and no big caves or glens in these valleys they could use. And that, that thing—it's in my mind that it probably needs some room as well. Bald Top, sir; we're almost straight west of it now."

Justin looked on the man with a keen eye, searching for signs of his character. "Born near here, you say. In the Domain or the Mark?"

"The Mark sir. In Cesmir. My family—"

"Not much love for the Emperor in those parts."

The man swallowed and stuttered, but his gaze held clear. "I won't lie—they hate the stubby little carker." Chuckles all around at this; "But I'm a soldier now, and I follow the flag. And you, sir." Justin smiled along with the dekentars—the man was not lying.

"Can you get to Bald Top from here?" Justin asked, and the man closed his eyes to think before answering with a nod.

"Best way's the south path, back up the road a bit; doesn't look like much but if you turn onto the right trail—"

"Sir," M'nesa said anticipating the course of the conversation. "They might not expect us to have local knowledge."

"And that creature ready to drop death as soon as they find us out." Justin's words fell like a hammer. The men shifted uncomfortably.

"Maybe it gets tired." "Or we could come on right after an attack—get a few minutes." "Have to try something, sir."

Justin turned to the local man. "Is there another way up?"

He shook his head, "Further north, but it's too small for horses, or even many men." After a moment he added, "Quicker, though—it means a real climb. It's up the back side of the mountain."

Justin stared down at his hands, and saw the ring which held his secret. From the swirl of his thought an idea bobbed to the surface. "Assemble the men. M'nesa, if you would, carry the flag with me."

The company stood, all that could stand, beyond the turned wagons, a shade over three score soldiers. They had marched and fought nearly three straight days. From inside the corral the wounded propped themselves up to listen. When Justin strode in front of them with the flag behind, they all saluted. Only then did Justin begin to think of the words he might say.

"Every man hopes for great things, if he is a man at all. We serve the Empire, and under its orders you have all done great things already. More will be required of you—and I have seen enough to tell me that you will answer well."

"But in the end, a man can only do the good he sees before him. We must not become lost in the desire to do more than what is asked in one day. Much rides with this flag, and on this mission. We risk … a great deal should it not reach Cryssigens. But first things first."

"I mean to destroy this band of robbers, tonight."

The cheer was unanimous. But the men greeted Justin's next orders with less enthusiasm.

"One dekent of cavalry with the wounded and all the mounts will ride south. Make as much noise as you can; I want these bastards to think they've bested us and we're retreating. Return when the sun is fully up and look for our signal. The rest, arm yourselves and prepare for combat on foot. Follow this officer who will guide you to the proper path. Move quietly and attack when you approach the top of the mountain."

"Dekentar Zetee commands in my absence. That is all."

Justin strode away to mutters and half-questions in his wake. As he prepared his gear, he could hear enough.

"Leaves us to fight—"

"Riding on alone, he'll never—"

"-bought-badge"

To M'nesa he spoke a few words quietly, then called over the North Mark dekentar to get the precise location of the northern path.

"Let me go with you sir!"

"You will lead the rest of the men by the southern way. I have your directions and the mountain will make itself known when I get closer."

"But—what do you plan to do?"

Justin motioned him closer as if in confidence, and knew the word would be passed the same way. "I mean to slay that monster."

$$\oplus \ \oplus \ \oplus$$

The most interesting thing about the Grog's Lees tavern in Cryssigens was not that it was still open, so late on the evening of the 12th. Located just off The Boards in a working-class precinct where folks needed their sleep, it sometimes closed an hour past dusk. But after a party or celebration, and most holidays, the lights were on well past midnight. Getting home after such a late night became each man's business.

The most interesting thing was not the vociferous complaints lodged about the drinks that Noudhal served up. Those too were quite usual, and on a night like tonight, any grousing about poisonous swill drowned beneath calls for refills. That would have been true, even if the patrons bought their own. Generally a cantankerous lot, but all in good fun, no harm done by talking.

Only one patron paid for all the drinks tonight in the Grog's Lees, and that was certainly unusual. The new fellow, just moved into the area from Tamar, stone merchant or some such, insisted this was the custom where he hailed. Not a single drinker there raised the smallest objection, and the mood on the whole remained buoyant. Simith, he said his name was; and that name was by far the most remarkable thing about the man.

But the truly interesting thing on this night of all nights, the famous bard Tambouri Shai had come to sing. The voice and fair face most often seen in noble houses, she who last year had filled the concert arena to the rafters, had elected by strange fate to sing on The Boards, for common folk who could pay only with applause. Tolerable drink tasted better when free, and when Tambouri sang, the cups were filled with a heavenly vintage.

"Give us 'The World Turned Upside-Down' then," one of the dock-loaders yelled. A chorus of boos answered this request; "I've heard enough verses of that lay to last my lifetime," added a tall one, and the grunt of affirmation he received was all the more meaningful coming from elves. "Heard enough about that carking usurper too," muttered an unseen patron and everyone banged their tankards to that.

"What then," asked Tambouri agreeably, her green eyes and silvery-blonde hair framing a dancing smile. "Shall I sing the love-song of the Dagniluviran for lonely men of the sea?" A gentle joke—what manly jack present would confess to loneliness among this crowd? "Sing us of the dragon-slayer, Provental," one suggested, and another, "Or the one about the monkey in the temple!" which brought a few laughs. Shai thought a moment with her fingers gently teasing rills from her instrument, then tilted her head back and began with yet another choice. She sang of Argens the Stargazer, his voyages to establish the empire in the days of legend, and of his many wives. This went down well. Of course, if Tambouri Shai had simply sung her own name over and over, many would have thought it fine. She could not sing a foul note, and besides, one could always just look at her.

Star and sea, first to be …

"So Giurid, what about the bricks you've owed me?"

"Owed your boss, you mean." The burly elf shot back. "I tell you what mine tells me—they're here when they come." Patrons rather dourly affirmed this state of affairs. The new fellow seemed to turn his head on a swivel, taking in shreds of similar conversations that blossomed under the music.

"-come not until Hawk, he tells me, and me with customers already so angry—"

"-angry I could eat stones, haven't seen wheat nor corn for a month, so I told him you can—"

"Can you believe? For a single bolt, and worsted at that—"

"-that scrawny thief and I dumped him in the river, I did. Guardsman fished him out and now he'll face trial. I can't wait."

"—weight in that scale, practically tips over with nothing in it! Crooked as a street in the Old City, I say."

"Say, don't wish your enemies to hell," the tall man bellowed over the music, "Just wait! Hell is coming here!" A huge cheer greeted this, laughter and another round.

A land, a home, 'cross sky and foam …

"Am I to understand," the new resident said, "that there's been some trouble with deliveries?"

"Hah!" said Giurid in reply, "Some trouble, in the same way this brew in my tankard is a bit sour! Hey Noudhal, where do you get a supply now that the new emperor's outlawed the poisoner's guild?"

The barkeep looked stoically into the man's mug and said, "It's just about empty, that dram of poison."

"Will you have another," the newcomer said politely, and the brick-loader nodded.

"So then, what is the problem? We had no difficulties in Tamar before I moved here."

"Tamar," a sailor said, "Nice solid Red House town. Cloth guilds, and a bit of the wood and stone. What did you say your business was?"

"Ceramic, mainly," the man said blandly, "and sometimes lime. You were saying?"

"Right, Tamar, Red House town. Everything in order there, no head-banging between the guild interests because they have the one boss, still in place. Here…" he paused to drink and ruminate, "more complicated."

"The Red House here too," a fat man added, "but the Blue, the Purple, Orange—they're all here. Took a lot to keep the guild interests under them all, em, orderly. But the Overlord, he was in charge."

"Right, now he's gone, everything's to hell. A man's delivery fails, and he makes it up by pinching someone else's. Or there's a fellow wants to sell in a new precinct, who's to stop him? The city guards wait for orders, mostly, the guilds are hiring their own."

"Prices up."

"Choices gone."

"Going to hell, that's what I said."

Struggle 'gainst demons fell, their secrets forced to tell …

"And crime," Giurid cried, "common folk canna' get safety nor justice while all the lords and ladies argue over who leads, who owns. You watch your pockets, friend," this to the man buying drinks, "your way home could be interesting."

"We can help him with that!" the sailor cried, "Let's not let him risk any funds, boys—another round!" Cheers and tankards extended, the new man's among them.

"Have there really been thefts?" he asked.

"Everywhere," a thin man attested, "even the wealthiest have had troubles—that's the reason they'll elect a new leader, I say."

"Did you hear what that brazen fellow did last week? You know the one, no one's seen him, he's got a name for a gem, like Jade, or Sard …"

"Feldspar!" several voices prompted at once.

"Aye, Feldspar. They say he stole the rod of office right from the Fire Grip's bedroom! The day before the big court proceeding."

"Nah, you've put it all wrong! The rod had already been stolen—this fellow took it back."

"A thief's a thief—"

"Says he's a stealthic."

"Oh and you've spoken to him? Or would know the difference between a thief and stealthic if the two of them ran you over?"

"Say that over here, little man, we'll see who gets run down in just a moment."

Tambouri, sensing a souring of the mood that would do no one good, switched her song in mid-chord and began to sing of the fabled stealthic Trekelny. Everyone enjoyed hearing how followers of Khoirah had been embarrassed, and the previous disagreement foundered and sank in mutual admiration of the fellow's exploits, aided of course by more ale.

The moon's shifting shadow was his friend,
He climbed the tower walls
All through the temple he did wend,
A' glide past guarded halls …

"It's clean and clear as fresh paint, we need the Overlord, and now," the sailor said and tankards banged, whether from agreement or for refills seemed less and less important.

"And that will happen, ah, the day past tomorrow?" the new resident guessed.

"Aye, second day from now's the Ides. In the arena, I hear."

"The arena! Why not the church, then?"

"'s'Closed, you fool," a woman muttered, and the new fellow looked confused to the point of dismay. Clearly matters in Cryssigens took serious turns.

"What Delith means," said Giurid, "is the Demonbender temple's closed. Ever since the stubby carker took over, you canna' worship where you would anymore." The grumbles of agreement at this were a bit less certain, not as unified.

"So," the new man puzzled, "that's where the investiture ceremony for the new Mark, the Overlord WOULD have taken place, but now …"

"Now, they canna' agree!" Giurid rejoined gleefully. "All the preachers, Hopeforgers, Stargazers, the Cryssians, those new ones, the name of that healer used to be outlawed …"

"Telhol," the new man put in helpfully.

"Telhol, is right. Say, your name again, friend?"

"Simith. Jonn Simith."

"Odd as three feet, that—but it's your fathers' fault, friend, not yours. Now the holy ones all argue over which is the highest and purest. Canna' agree, there's a wonder."

"So," the woman carried on, whose arms spoke of work in a smithy, "the arena, because it's between, and big. They want everyone to see it."

"Ya, and we can go for free!" put in another, bringing grunts of surprise, "I heard it myself, free admission on the side seats for any citizen. They'll have a quick vote, and crown the new Overlord right there."

"How exciting," Simith said, though he seemed less than overwhelmed. Perhaps the size of his bar bill was beginning to worry him. But he loyally said, "A toast, then, to our new Overlord, and may it bring the end of all our troubles."

"Still," he mused when the toast was through, and two or three more of the same ilk after it, "Is it certain they'll have the vote on the Ides? Who's the new Overlord to be, then?"

No one knew, though many offered opinions; the head of their guild, or house, or church, all were bandied about. The smith suggested the widow of the former Mark, though it was unprecedented. "And the vote," the new man persisted, "does it have to be on the Ides? I seem to recall a custom, the emperor may have a representative at these moots."

"No emperor's man at this table," the sailor said knowingly. All heads turned to him. "The righteous carker's not going to make it."

Exclamations from all sides, including cheers and questions together. Tambouri stopped with a smile and shake of her head, hopeless to sing against such news. The new man, noticing, stepped over and said a few words, even handing her a tip. Meanwhile, the sailor had all attention at the bar.

"I'm just this hour in from Cesmir," he said knowingly. "My captain sets out with half a cargo loaded, right after a horseman comes pounding down to the docks with a message for him. He says nothing to me, mind—but by halfway here, the news gets around through the crew." The man leaned in as if telling a secret to only one, but his voice carried through the silence.

"The emperor sent a man, alright, flag and horsemen and trumpeter and all. But he won't make it. Stuck in the hills south, he is. Waylaid by bandits."

"What happened!"

"Destroyed, as I hear it," the sailor said matter of factly. "Or shortly to be. But that was yesterday, the 11th, and no one had reached the barony by evening, I'll attest." All agreed none except a fast post rider could make the city in two days. And the posts, they weren't so reliable since the Overlord was slain.

"If the emperor's vote isn't at the table, you mark me," Giurid concluded, "these lords of ours, who won't agree on which direction heaven lies, will be all agreed in the arena before the whole city. We'll have a unanimous vote, and a new Mark by the evening of the Ides."

"Well," the new man replied coming back to the bar, "that would seem to settle matters nicely. I'm for sleep, ladies and gentlemen; I thank you for indulging my custom, and making me feel so welcome in your precinct. Shall we toast once more to the new Overlord of the North Mark, whoever it may be?"

Everyone agreed the new fellow was welcome in the Grog's Lees whenever he saw fit, and many promises were made to return the drinks he had bought all round. "I shall be drunk for a year," he murmured quietly, and got a round of laughs and huzzahs. Curiously, instead of paying out coin he signed a piece of paper with the barkeep, and then took his leave.

"Noudhal, what's that then?" Giurid remarked, "Did he leave you with the bill?"

"Not a bit of it," the barkeep scoffed, "This is the new way of doing business, don't you know anything? He has a letter of credit with me. Damned to the hells if I know how it works, but when I take this signed chit to the bank, the coin's hard and real, that I swear to."

"Do you mean he carries no coins?" the brick-loader cried in disbelief. "Here then, minstrel Shai, what coin did he give you?"

Smiling and shaking her head slightly, the beautiful bard held up a small gemstone, rusty and mottled, well polished but of no particular beauty.

"Doesn't seem like much for all your work, mistress?"

"Oh I rather like it," she replied demurely. "He said it could bring me luck."

⊕ ⊕ ⊕

With both moons up, Justin easily made out the landmarks his man recited. The oak, the gulch, the split rock—all large items hard to miss and unlikely to change with the years. This country was wild and even by himself Justin moved slowly. Furta rode with the company, and publicly Justin gave out that he expected to rendezvous with them all by mid-morning. Only M'nesa heard his true purpose, as Justin left him the flag of mission and his instructions to continue.

Justin had little hope that he could ever defeat this creature, whatever it was. He only thought to draw it away, or perhaps wound it, distract the thing so that the attack could succeed. He slipped through the glades and across slanted rock-faces, constantly ascending as the trail wound around to the northern face of the mountain looming above. The closer he came, the more he was convinced that Bald Top indeed held the bandit lair. The top half of the mountain was practically clear in all directions and the summit looked as if a giant knife had sliced across the crown of a bread-crust. It was the spot he would choose; but then, he would never leave the approaches unwatched. His man had no idea where the lookouts might be, but as Justin came ever closer to the last ascent, he saw no sign.

And then came a better one, his first stroke of luck. He noticed a stand of brush, between two trees across a stream, that seemed a bit too perfect. Circling to one side, he could see a hunting blind, constructed as cover, and empty. So the guards stood here; had they been killed in the fighting? Or perhaps they deserted, as he might have done. Skeer clearly set his monster to attack his own men along with his enemy. Justin's plan depended in large part on striking while that mistake was still fresh.

Bandit lords ruled by fear—any bond of obedience backed by his threat of death dissolved after such a betrayal. That and wealth were all he could offer as long as times weren't too bad. Now, Skeer's men would probably filter away back to the farms and woodcotes, where the work was harder, the drinks fewer, and life more assured. In time: yet Justin could not afford to wait for his enemy to lose by attrition. More than likely it was already too late. More than likely, he mused grimly, he would die before sun-up. But the good he could see beckoned him.

He moved a bit faster now, hoping the guards had all lapsed, and soon reached the base of the north face. His man had never been here himself, and the trail he spoke of led no further, so Justin was on his own. He paced about scanning above and seeking the best approach.

Making a choice, he hitched his sword around to the back for greater ease of climbing, and started up. Almost immediately, the way grew too steep for two feet; a few narrow paths a goat might have used, but Justin needed both hands on the thin sapling-trunks thrusting sideways from the rocky soil. Small shrubs, thick with branches and sometimes thorns, they had stubborn roots, always in reach and as useful as the rungs of a ladder. In a short time, he was several hundred feet above the valley floor. Stopping to rest and mop his face, Justin turned to look out a long way under the twin moonlight.

There was no sound and nothing moved. Justin felt the deep peace of this wild country, and reflected that many of the men in Skeer's band had probably been just loners, roving these hills and acknowledging no lord. His man, but for some unknown twist of fate, might have become one of them. He took in the pine-scented air, the breath of night, and kept scanning for movement by moonlight. Not men, Justin looked for deer; he wished he had brought his bow.

With a start, he realized his mind had wandered far. What was he doing here, seriously thinking of taking to the life of an unknown yeoman? A languid sense stole over him, here away from too-tight schedules, impossible orders, from the noises of the company and the burdens of command. Justin recalled he had not been alone in more than half a year, had never considered what he might want only for himself.

For himself, Justin realized, he could indeed stay, and hunt, and live free of the world. He would never accomplish either mission, now: in deciding to attack this camp he guaranteed that he would fail to reach Cryssigens by the Ides. Without him, the barons, preachers and guildmasters of the city would vote for an Overlord who would lead the North Mark against the empire. None of them could know what strength waited to crush insurrection—the Mark, already weakened after Viridian's overthrow, held no answer to the power of the new military that Hansen wielded.

All because Justin had failed. No use to blame others—the flag and the ring had come to him, and Justin in his soul had wanted them both. And so he climbed the mountain alone, to face a monster and die. Perhaps he sought to wash out his failures with his blood. Perhaps Valin had done the same.

But to live alone … What would it be like, to rise when you wished, eat when hungry, take nothing away from any lord, have no impact on other men?

The men, he thought, that was the key. Perhaps there was no career of honor to which he could return. A life without meaning might be far from unpleasant. But in an hour, more or less, men following his commands would attack the south face of the bandit camp. If he left now no one would find him; assuming his death, men would speak of his brave and doomed attempt, and maybe the family name, if not the line, would recover. It only required that Justin become just like Skeer, and leave his men to die.

The inner fight was over before Justin knew it had started. Something snapped into place, like the plates on Tass's cestus, and all of it came rushing back—the meaning, the orders, the burden his spirit rose to with fierce joy. Other men could be happy this way—perhaps some of those above him, if they lived, would return to it. Justin wished them well, as he resumed the climb.

On the last few furlongs of sheer vertical stone, Justin had to hunt for foot and handholds, rising only ten feet a minute. He was happy for his thick gauntlets, a bit less so for the stylish cavalry boots. But he managed not to make too much noise as he worked his way up and ever up. He began to smell something fearsome and unknown, the stench of the beast, easily overwhelming the mundane odors of cookfires and trash. As he reached for a new handhold, Justin's foot slipped and his face pressed flat against the stone. The friction almost knocked his helmet off, and when he drew his hand back to hold it on, he nearly fell. Gyring frantically from the waist and balanced on one foot, he managed, barely, to hang on. Getting his four limbs back into place, Justin thought of the storied exploit of the stealthic Trekelny, who ascended the tower of Khoirah and stole the Horn of the Serpent. Or so the bards sang; that would be a valuable man to have in his company, he mused. Certainly he would do better than a disgraced captain with no clear plan for his next five minutes.

At the very top of the cliff, Justin received his second spot of fortune. The place he neared, reeking strongly of something unearthly and foul, did not look down into the bowl of the summit at once. Expecting a trash-midden, Justin eased his head over the rampart and saw at once that another wall of sorts stood a rod or so away. Beyond it, the rest of the summit was blocked from view, and the space within formed a kind of enclosure, inky dark, perhaps for horses. The sounds of the bandit camp came plainly now, he could hear muttered words, and the trudge of guards on the opposite side. Evidently they thought this back cliff not worth watching, as no large group could come up it. With infinite care he eased his body over and lowered himself within, dropping less than a foot to the ground. There, his good fortune ended.

He nearly passed out at once. The stench, lying closer to the earth inside this space, was enough to make his eyes water. Justin almost turned his ankle when he landed, one foot slipping inside some kind of post-hole or knot in the ground. But he dared not move, as he quietly gasped and tried to maintain his balance. The moons above cast shadows over most of this space, but their movement slowly revealed more on his side as he stood there straining to see. Justin became increasingly sure that the opposite, darker side of the enclosure held … something. Not horses, not a midden; he had come down directly into the creature's lair. That explained the lack of guards.

He reached over-shoulder and silently drew his blade, only now shifting his foot out of the post-hole. The sides of it moved a little, and he heard a clank like metal. Looking down, he could see other post-holes revealed by the light of the moon, a line of wrought iron leading back into the darkness. Chains. With links the size of his boot, as thick as his wrist. Without knowing how, Justin sensed the monster was awake, and watching him.

He had staked all on the idea that it was not a dragon. Even a young one would have been impossible for any but a great mage to control even briefly. And dragon scales were impenetrable, according to legend; yet Skeer had kept this beast high in the air, beyond the range of arrows, or its rocks would have torn the company to flinders. So it could be hurt; he deemed that prize worth his life. And he would never order another man to face this. He held his sword and waited, hoping his knees could stay solid until the fight began. After that—only waiting made things hard for a military man.

The chains dragged nearly taut and he heard the hiss of the creature as it stood. Justin tensed for the spring, the attack, maybe one chance to do it an injury. But many moments passed, in an agony of suspense, before anything happened. Slowly, so slowly he wasn't sure if the creature moved or the moons pushed the shadows back, a head emerged from the darkness. A foot higher than his head, its hard beak and piercing, ferocious eyes glared at him from five steps away. He saw one foreleg, the size of a tree trunk and tipped with five talons the length of scimitars, gripping the raw stone. Like a stork stalking in a frog-pond, the monster took a single, slow step closer, looking intently at Justin as if there were something behind him. Now he could make out the rippling, muscular golden skin on its door-sized chest, and a corona of feathers behind its head. It suddenly flipped its wings into view, gorgeous multi-colored sails that brushed both walls of the enclosure; Justin stumbled back a step and half-cried out in alarm. But the monster did not press any advantage, though the chain clearly reached him; a random thought came to Justin's mind doubting it would even hold.

Time continued passing, leaving Justin alive and with decisions to make. The beast was so powerful, so magnificent, it stunned him and halved his sense of purpose. Looking for an opening, Justin tilted his head slightly to one side: at once, the monster did the same, so like a parrot or a watching crow. It hissed breath in and out, but had not screamed. In an instant, Justin recognized the legend he beheld was a gryphon. And as it continued to stare directly at him, he realized also, that the emblem on his helmet was not that of a hawk.

He realized his jaw was hanging open when he saw the gryphon doing the same thing. The ground of combat was shifting under his feet, and other details, exposed by the moonlight, built a picture in his mind that led down a different path from the one that sold his life. If the creature forebore to attack him, he might hold the door here throughout the assault, prevent the bandits from using it. Better yet, if he could open the north gate entrance to the lair, he could save a dozen lives or more.

The inner wall of this enclosure was a row of close-set tree-trunks driven into the ground like a stockade, but he could see between cracks large enough to put an arm through. Stepping carefully to one side while facing his head towards the beast, Justin edged to the posts and glanced sideways into the camp. The glimpses told him much: guttered campfires burned unattended, sleeping forms scattered about, less than six men on the south face barricade, and everywhere a sense of utter exhaustion. He grinned to think of the toll his troops had taken. Where was M'nesa with the men?

He reached around the door-post to unlatch the gate when he heard a woman's muffled scream and snapped his head around to look. Two men dragged a struggling form between them toward a nearby cave mouth several yards down the north face. Justin looked first at the monster—still holding its position—then at the south gate, and back to the cave where the trio disappeared. The good he could see—that was all. Justin slipped through the timber door.

At once the mountaintop resounded with the scream of the creature, and the bandits jerked from sleep in terror. Keeping his wits about him despite the mistake, Justin loped low by the wooden wall and entered the cave. Lanterns nailed to the rock revealed a scene of horror; two bandits held the gagged woman down over a stoney spur, while a third, larger villain hefted an axe. Beyond the humans lurked a horror perhaps four feet high, seemingly made of living reddish stone and scuttling near the thick metal bars of its cage on three legs. The first bandit became aware of the intruder too late to save his life, and Justin felt only unfettered joy as he ran him through. The other man dropped the woman, clawed briefly at his waist for the knife, then fled. The leader, surely Skeer Two-Eye, barked an oath in surprise but engaged gamely.

The foes clashed and parried in the narrow cave, at first to the backdrop of a woman's sobs and scrabbling retreat, then to the awful chittering impatience of the caged demon. Skeer wielded the battle-axe more like a hatchet, and despite his girth was shifty-quick. Still, he had never encountered a man of imperial training one on one: all the science of fighting—the advantages of a step closer to an obstacle or a double-feint's gain—all that lay with Justin. The screech of the gryphon came again, echoing redoubled inside the cave to make both fighters grimace, but they battled on. Now there were other shouts, the bratch of a broken gate, men dying and the clash of steel.

Skeer's face fell as he divined their meaning. With a scorching oath he came on in a flurry to finish his enemy. Justin parried the first whistling blow, and nearly deflected the second, but the glancing blade scraped past the end of the sword into his upper arm. The chain shirt absorbed a bit more of the force, but his bicep took the rest in a keen kiss through the uniform sleeve. Maintaining his balance, Justin switched grips and brought his sword around in a lethal arc, straight through the bandit's neck. His dead body staggered back from the force of the blow, its trunk falling limply against the rocky spur.

Clutching his arm, Justin started to turn back to assist his men when he became aware of an eerie presence. Wheeling, he saw the demon squatting down as its legs seemed to drink in the fountaining blood from the bandit's body. Above its blind head, a patch of mist formed, and in it a human shape showed dimly. Justin came three steps closer to the cage with every hair on end.

"Report," came the nameless tone. Justin wondered if he could be seen, and quickly shattered a lantern with his blade to halve the light.

"Report, Skeer!"

So that was the way of it. Everywhere he looked, men following orders. Justin could no longer feel the pain in his arm, the blood trickling down, as he began to shake with outrage. Demon sacrifice, monstrous creatures, mystical forces beyond the ken of lawful beings, all ranged against him. No, worse—against the vision of a lawful land, free of Despair. Against the flag of mission.

"Is the captain dead?" the voice insisted.

"Aye," Justin said in a fey mood, "Valin T'lenthor is dead, thanks to you."

"You shall have your reward," the voice assured.

"As shall you, I swear by Argens," Justin returned, raising his blade.

"Who is—" the voice demanded, but the death-squeal of the lesser demon made the misty image disappear as if it too had been pierced. From the bandit-leader's corpse, Justin's eye caught the glint of a long-handled crop with an emerald studded pommel; things were beginning to make sense.

Outside the cave, chaos reigned. Soldiers poured over the barricade, and the bandits had no opportunity to respond with bows which were their principal weapons. After fighting with imperial soldiers, their numbers advantage had shrunk—from three to one two days ago, to less than even odds. Not a fair fight, and they knew it. The gryphon, lunging through the open door, had reached a man-length into the camp on the end of its massive chain and bitten two of its captors in half. The rest now gave it a wide berth. Justin's appearance from their leader's cave was the final straw—every robber that had the space threw down his weapon; the manual directed that quarter be granted except on direct orders.

When the men cheered Justin in victory, they were cut off by the gryphon's scream. Following his instinct, Justin took the crop in hand and stepped before the group to approach it. Stifled cries of warning behind him, he came within ten feet, though the beast was at the end of its chain with only the hindquarters still in the enclosure. Regarding him closely, the beast again remained quiet and still, though tense and seemingly angry that it could not rage. Justin felt the sky lightening in the east, dawn on the 13th Dolphin. On this side of the enclosure he saw a massive leather saddle, prods on spear handles, a silver bit, and wide studded reins. Justin stepped closer, closer, beyond the corpses and within sword's reach of its massive beak. Still it only stared at him, as soldier and bandit alike held breath. He reached up one hand, and the gryphon opened its beak, showing a sharp tongue inside and reeking of eaten meat. Justin withdrew the hand, then sharply snapped the crop across its forehead as the men cried out in fear. The gryphon reared its head back, but did not attack or scream. Stepping back, Justin turned to address the men. He could see at a glance that they were his now, and would follow him anywhere.

"Your dekentars will recruit up to strength, and officer Zetee is in command. The plunder of this camp is at his discretion. Any prisoners here will be freed at once; the lives of these bandits are all forfeit to the empire. Leave them in the custody of the Baron in Cesmir."

"March north with all due speed, along the coast road to Cryssigens. I expect to see you there on the 16th or 17th at the latest."

"The flag of mission goes with me."

Justin exchanged final orders with the dekentars, saw to the newly wounded troops, and took a moment to relieve M'nesa of some of the money in Valin's old treasury. The men greeted the morning with fervor, fueled by victory and bandit victuals. Time sped by, nearly noon before all was set in order. Far too late now.

Two volunteers and one of the bandits who had done it before saddled the creature while Justin stayed near its head. With the reins in one hand and the gryphon eyeing him like something good to eat, he approached its side and kept all his experience of unruly horses in mind. When he sat, the creature tensed a long moment, and Justin realized it was expecting to be struck. Risking his grip, he reached down and stroked its forearm-long feathers a bit, with no change. Making sure of the leg-straps and belt, he uttered a brief prayer to Argens, took a deep breath, and gave a sharp kick. "Hai!"

He was aloft in a heartbeat, higher at once than the mountaintop; already the men below were tiny figures waving and cheering. In the morning sun he could see leagues in every direction. He struggled a bit with the enormous strength of the beast, but his equestrian training, no doubt aided by the helmet and the crop, were working in his favor. As he turned north, the flag of mission snapped in the rushing wind and he heard a dim echo of the soldiers below.

> *They tell us nothing of this job*
> *WHAT ELSE, WE'RE SOLDIERS NOW*
> *Just us, we'll lay the northern mob*
> *Clap-Clap! BUT NEVER QUESTION HOW*
> *And while we fight, left high and dry*
> *Guess who with the courtesans will lie*
> *We've the finest captain gold can buy*
> *AND THE WORLD'S TURNED UPSIDE-DOWN*

The Ides of the Dolphin was a brilliant day filled with sunshine and the promise of spring. Cryssigens turned out in all its finest, streaming by the main boulevards to the arena, which had been closed to gladiatorial games since New Years two winters ago. The guards had almost more than they could handle, when the rumor spread that the open seating was filled and no one else would be admitted. It wasn't true, but bad news is a stubborn thing, and some later told of guards who abandoned their posts so as not to miss out on the sights.

There were plenty of those. In the center sections on both sides of the oval, a rainbow of colors greeted the eye as the various Houses of the North Mark sat together; Red and Blue closest to the central, empty dais, Purple and Orange across the arena from them, and the lesser hues to each side. The House Cups, one leader from each of the colors sat at the enormous damasked table in the arena center, and each leading dignitary of the city come to join them had a parade. The arena floor had been groomed and strewn with rose petals, and scented misters wielded by the attendants created an atmosphere that folks found unforgettable, though the day's vote lay still ahead.

The Patriarch of the church of Argens Hopeforger came on foot though he was venerable in years; folks murmured that he wasn't wearing the ancient headpiece given to the Highforge of Cryssigens, but perhaps he was just being humble. That would be a first, many snickered. The High Priestess of the Stargazers came in a litter headed by dancing acolytes and manly guards; the stadium held its collective breath, waiting for the first sight of her, and cheered wildly when she stepped forth dressed in brilliant purple, flowing, but not at all concealing. A good thing she had not walked, the men said, or there would have been a riot.

The high priests of the other sects of Argens entered next, some with cymbals and others with gold-clad guards. Last in line was a tall ascetic from the Devouting Sinter, the monastery to the east where it was whispered the holy men still worked great miracles. Amid the hubbub, a plain-dressed preacher with beard and long unstyled hair entered by a small gate used for the fighters and sat far from the empty Overlord's chair. The curate of the chapel to Telhol, as peaceful as his hero, took his seat while everyone was watching the feudal lords who came together. Still, he had a full vote like these others.

By the main gate used for the larger arena beasts, the lords of the Mark entered together, the Barons of Cesmir and Gaden side by side followed by their retinue. The Fire Grip of Cryssigens, leader of the city guard and second in command only to the Overlord, came after, though he was the Barons' equal in rank. This was a good sign, many nodded, that the leaders were in accord; the blue sash and sapphire ring proclaiming his House tie was bold but not out of fashion. The Baron of Tralmachia, as ever, was absent and so forfeit his right to have a say. Besides his chair, that of the Master of Horse would also be empty, slain in the rebellion along with the Overlord Kreel and not yet filled.

There were many more, of course, lords and guildmasters and city officials, all with less than one vote each. They arranged themselves around the massive table in a pattern that suggested their loyalties, and prepared to calculate the ballot as if there were a point. No one in the common seats knew what choice their leaders had made. But anything was better than the disorder they had suffered these past eight months and more. Looking at the last empty seat, down at the end reserved for the representative of the emperor, told them all they needed to know. Nothing complicated about a unanimous vote.

The Patriarch was only half-way through his opening prayer when the chaos struck.

First the morning sun flickered, as if the day had blinked. Then thousands of people hit the earth or sought the space beneath the benches, as the horrendous screech of the creature tore the air. Hardened warriors dropped their weapons, hundreds fainted and fragments of panic prevailed everywhere.

Out of the open sky dropped a creature from a beautiful nightmare, its enormous talons churning the earth of the arena and kicking up plumes of red petals like a shower of promised blood. On the monster's back sat a warrior with a silver helm and bearing the flag of the empire. Surveying the table group, he dismounted with expert skill, and momentarily sagged with weariness or perhaps drunkenness. But he straightened and advanced fearlessly past the sharp beak of his mount to address the group. As the creature swiveled its head towards the loudest noises in the arena, things soon quieted down from all quarters so that any could hear him.

"Greetings, lords and ladies all. I am Captain Justin Thyme, appointed representative of the Son of the Sun Yula himself, deputed to attend these proceedings and claim my vote in the selection of your next Overlord."

Complete silence reigned in Cryssigens. Justin quickly scanned as many of the leading faces as he could, trying to discern mere surprise from knowing disappointment. Maintaining his face a mask, he belied none of the surging disquiet in his soul, as he sought to focus, stay sharp (or even awake) and complete his second mission to the ruin of the first.

"Has the vote yet been taken?" he asked with a touch too much eagerness. Into the stony silence, only the curate of Telhol dropped an answer, simply "No, Captain, you are truly named." With a gentle smile, he gestured, "Will you sit?"

"It might be best," Justin replied, "if I kept hold of these reins a while." He watched as noble, wealthy faces gulped in apprehension. He smiled, and noting their sour reactions seized upon his best course. The image of Valin T'lenthor came to his mind, not in dying, but as he saw him in their earlier life. He was, after all, the man for this mission; and who knew how to play him better?

Putting on a sneer and planting the flag beside him, Justin said "On the orders of our emperor, I move for a delay in the voting." A susurration of disapproval from the arena crowd grew louder like a tide, and he looked up for a moment at the teeming, colorful four-score thousand, who stood against him in hatred. At the noise, the gryphon screamed again and once more the crowd quieted. Turning back, Justin presented the crop and rapped the gryphon sharply across the beak, which brought a round of squeals and cries even from the table. The creature reared its head back, cawed, met his gaze, and then suddenly crouched thunderously to the ground. Justin whispered a quick prayer of thanks to Argens for rewarding his audacity, and spun back to the table, daring to let go the reins.

"As per the ancient practices of the empire and this Mark, I vote to delay the proceedings by the customary period." He held his breath a moment, taking in the group who stared poison back at him, and then added, "Do not trouble to name candidates, now, therefore—in the absence of better acquaintance I intend to vote against any and all."

The lords and preachers of Cryssigens took in this unpleasant development and their faces began to change. Glances cast in various directions, uncertainty, shifting loyalties—Justin could sense but not yet log any of it in those moments. Whatever they had agreed before today was changed; second and third choices might be dearer. But the main thing, this vote was delayed. The North Mark, against its will, had been given a chance to survive.

"You have this right," intoned the Patriarch of Argens Hopeforger stiffly, "and we will honor it. The council of election is adjourned until the Ides of the Dragon in two months' time, at which day we WILL select a new Overlord. By majority vote," he added with meaning.

"In the meantime," asked the elf dressed completely in red, "what do you expect us to do with—with this creature?"

Justin looked as cool as he envisioned Valin would be, and said nonchalantly, "Let it stay here, where there is plenty of room. If there are any that can supply it with meat, I am of course empowered to pay." A second's pause, after he dangled this bait, and then the fish began to bite. "I will be delighted to supply you," said a man in guilder's garb, cutting off two others who had also started to speak. Justin noted all three of them, but was distracted by a woman's voice.

"And what of you, Captain? Will you take rest somewhere in our fair city?" The priestess in purple was undoubtedly the most attractive woman Justin had ever seen; he stopped his jaw on its way agape and managed to say, "Perhaps—it would be best if I quartered here tonight, your, em, holiness." Even the leaders of the city could not repress their chuckles at his choice of title, and Justin struggled to regain the upper hand. "My steed is not fully comfortable alone, and I believe this arena can serve no better purpose in the next two months than as a bivouac for my men."

"You brought armed men into this Mark?" a knight demanded with anger. Justin knew how to answer this.

"Aye, and almost not enough. My company is marching north with all due speed and will be here on the morrow," he claimed confidently. "I was forced to go ahead because soldiers of the lawful empire were attacked here in the Mark." Justin maintained the arrogant mask of derision he remembered from Valin as he scanned their faces for reaction—who knew, who surprised, who admired the attempt and who cheered its failure?

These were clever opponents, and he saw only glints and guesses, none yet with names. Losing control, Justin stepped to the table and planted his fists on the cloth. "One of you," he hissed, "is guilty of treason against the Empire. Before these two months are up, by Argens, I will find you out and bring you to justice."

There was little anyone could say to that, and the council broke up before a throng too fascinated to be disappointed. Justin stayed behind, standing straight as a rod and not looking at all like a man who had flown for two-score hours without a break. The empty arena even under mid-day light struck him as the loneliest place he'd ever been. His mount slept like the dead, and Justin was alone. He could hardly have been more tired, as he trudged to the central chair of the vacant table and sat.

But his heart was full of that nameless emotion that mixed one part pride with one part satisfaction and a dram or two of reckless joy. Feeling that indeed he had fulfilled his orders, he slumped in the throne of the Overlord of the North Mark and stared at the flag of mission. Planted in the earth where men had died for amusement, it tossed its banner in the gentle breeze like a spirited horse, sensing adventures, risk, and more of this feeling in the days to come. Captain Justin fell asleep and dreamed of the orders not yet given.

GLOSSARY

Altair Way	street	main thoroughfare of Cryssigens
Ancient	language	tongue of the heroes, dragons and beings of power; mortals may not lie when using it
Areghel	hero	first king of the Percentalion, hero of martial wizards
Argens	city	capital city of the Southern Empire, on the central western coast, named for its hero
Argens Demonbender		hero-aspect, major form of devotion to Argens, currently outlawed, emphasizing sorcerous lore and mastery of demons
Argens Hopeforger		hero-aspect, major form of devotion to Argens, emphasizing courage, light and leadership
Argens Stargazer		hero-aspect, major form of devotion to Argens, emphasizing foresight and love
Argensian Empire		aka the Southlands, vast Elven Empire established by Argens, capital city also named Argens
Astor	hero	Perilsgroom, hero of Stealthics from ancient days
Bald Top	mountain	small loaf-shaped mountain the border hills
Battle of Broken Chains		Dolphin 2001 ADR, first victory of the rebellion over Loyalist forces of the North Mark
Battle of the Razor		pivotal battle of ancient times, Despair was ejected from the Lands forever in the year 0 ADR
Battle of Tor Perite		site of decisive battle (Serpent, 2001 ADR) that defeated Viridian XXVII and put Yula I on the throne of Argens
Bedou-uu	race	desert dwelling nomads of the Shimmering Mindsea
bought badge	phrase	insulting term for an officer who purchased a commission he could not earn
Brow of the Ecclesiast		artefact, mystic crown with fabulous powers, burns the unworthy wearer

centar		unit of soldiers, ten dekents = 100 men
Cesmir	barony	southern barony of the North Mark
cestus	weapon	spiked metal glove used by gladiators
Charnel Testing		an attempt to wear the Brow of the Ecclesiast, which results in death by burning for the unworthy
Conar	city	capital of the kingdom of Men, named for its hero
Cryssians	sect	devotees of Cryss Altair
Cryssigens	city	capital city of the North Mark, wealthy and Color-ful
Dagnaluviran	song	heroic tale of love between Dagnar and Elosira
dekent		unit of soldiers, one dekent equals ten men (led by a dekentar)
dekentar		junior officer's rank in the army or guards
Devouting Sinter		monastery of holy men in Gaden, bordering the Shimmering Mindsea
Earthcut River		runs through Gaden and Cesmir to the Western Sea
Ekhonon	hero	second son of Conar, judgement and architecture
Exemplars	hero	minor heroes of ancient times
Far Mark		recently recolonized duchy of the Argensian Empire, next to the Swords of Stone
Fire Grip	title	City Commander of Cryssigens, regent of the Mark in the absence of the Overlord
Flame of the First		mild oath, reference to Argens who caught a slice of the Sun in his hand
Gaden	barony	east-central barony of the North Mark
Gelvorging Deep		thick forested area, unsettled and hiding bandits or monsters
glassteel		clear substance harder than metal
Grog's Lees	tavern	modest, in The Boards neighborhood of Cryssigens
Highforge	title	rank given to the Preacher worthy of the Brow of the Ecclesiast
Horn of the Serpent		relic of those devoted to Khoirah the Betrayer, stolen by Trekelny and now lost (*see Three Minutes to Midnight*)

House Cups	title	heads of various Colors in Cryssigens, wielding great wealth and influence
Ides of the Dolphin		date, mid-point of the 2nd month, 15th
Imperial Domain		barony, gorgeous settled lands adjacent to Argens and direct vassalage to the Emperor
Insectir	monster	giant bug creatures, repugnant to Elves
intakta volar	language	in Ancient: I wish for healing
kemetaria	feature	burial ground, a Despairing practice to put bodies under the earth instead of cremation
Khoirah	anti-hero	the Betrayer, third son of Conar who treated with Despair in ancient times
lith	drug	performance enhancing, addictive, poisonous
Ma-Eldar	hero	Hopelord of Elves, father of Argens
Master of Horse		leader of all Imperial cavalry
North Mark		northern duchy of Argens, with a history of rebellion; capital city Cryssigens
noun-chakas	weapon	two wooden hafts connected by a few links of chain
Nubian	race	tall black Men living in the Southern jungle, fearsome warriors
odd as three feet		phrase, reference to demonic creatures, meaning something is very strange or unexpected
Old City		northeastern quarter of Cryssigens, once wealthy but long since abandoned
Overlord	title	aka North Mark, title of the ruler of that duchy
Palace of the Sun		castle, Emperor's dwelling in Argens' capital
Patriarch	title	church leader in a nation or great city
pentadek		unit of soldiers, five dekents = 50 men
piazzo		center of abandoned Old Cryss, open paved area with temples and more
Ring of Peace	miracle	Telholian invocation creating a no-magic, no-violence zone
Salva Way		bordering the piazzo in Old Cryss
Scapegrace Street		bordering the piazzo in Old Cryss

Shard Demon	monster	held prisoner beneath the palace in Cryssigens
Shimmering Mindsea		large sandy desert between Argens and the Swords of Stone
silversteel		magical metal, unbreakable and rare
somnos	drug	induces sleep
Son of the Sun	title	honorific title for the Emperor, successor to Argens
strategos	title	senior officer's rank in the army or guard
Sun Throne		Emperor's throne in Argens, also a reference to the Emperor's rank
Tamar	city	small trading city about a day's journey from Cryssigens
Telhol	hero	fourth son of Conar, hero of peace and healing
Tepid River		separates Cryssigens from the Old City on its way to the Western Sea
The Boards		poor neighborhood in Cryssigens bordering the River Cryss
Tralmachia	barony	northernmost barony of the North Mark, mountainous and isolated
Viper	sect	secret police under Viridian, now outlawed

SHARDS OF LIGHT II: FENCING REPUTATION

A Sword and Sorcery novel from the Lands of Hope.

When the elven lords, preachers and merchants of Cryssigens need wrongs righted without clues, they look for the stealthic Feldspar to solve their problems. But the legend without a face is hard to find: and when Feldspar takes a commission from the most famous, and beautiful, priestess in the city, he finds problems of his own piling up, and is forced to choose between Hope and safety.

available as eBook and in print
ISBN 978-3-95681-095-4

SHARDS OF LIGHT III: PERILOUS EMBRACES

A Sword and Sorcery novel from the Lands of Hope.

As the city of Cryssigens spirals towards chaos, its leaders scheme in secret to alter the future. But W'starrah Altieri, priestess of Argens Stargazer, already sees it. Can she balance her loyalty to the North Mark against the threat of an imperial invasion, and locate the mystic artefact whose touch will either unite the land in peace or end her life in fire? And what chance, in all this tumult, for the most beautiful woman in the kingdom to find the love of her life before Argens requires her death?

Coming soon

SHARDS OF LIGHT IV: SHARDS OF LIGHT

A Sword and Sorcery novel from the Lands of Hope.

The North Mark teeters toward a rebellion that will bring crushing retribution from the Argensian Empire. Only three heroes, barely acquainted and scattered far, have the chance between them to avert war and ruin. Can Captain Justin escape the death-trap of Tralmachia and return in time for the crucial vote? Does Feldspar have the skill and courage to revisit the Old City and snare the fabled Brow of the Ecclesiast from its current home among bandits and Bugs? Will W'starrah Altieri, beautiful priestess who hired the stealthic and loves the soldier, see into the conspiracy's heart before the wave of fire she has foreseen engulfs her and the city of Cryssigens? The fate of a kingdom is reflected in these mortal Shards of Light.

Coming soon

Judgement's Tale: The Omnibus

Two millenia of peace are coming to an end.

For twenty centuries the Lands of Hope prospered from their Heroes' peace, but suffer now from their absence. Chaos grows in the central kingdom of the Lands of Hope known as the Percentalion. Even the bravest adventurers seem unable to travel in or out safely. The sundered populations are trapped there, beyond communication and without hope.

Worse yet, the liche Wolga Vrule plots escape from his extra-worldly prison to unleash a tide of undeath, and enlists the Earth Demon Kog, who ruled the Percentalion millennia ago, as an uneasy ally.

On the western coast of the Lands of Hope, Solemn Judgement comes ashore, having journeyed with his father across the ocean. Solemn arrives both a stranger and and orphan, driven to complete the lore his father died to give him. Will he discover Wolga Vrule's plan in time to prevent the return of Despair?

continues in "Eye of Kog"

THE PLANE OF DREAMS

A standalone novel from the Lands of Hope

In the southern empire of Argens just roiled by the rebellion of Yula, a band of adventurers returns from the Shimmering Mindsea bearing enormous treasure and minus one of its members. The Tributarians, unaware of the growing threat to the waking world, embark on separate plans. But the spirit of the hero lives on in all of them, as their good deeds have consequences beyond their original intention. Will it be enough to avert the peril they have unwittingly brought about?

This first epic-length tale set in the Lands of Hope features a complex world and intelligent, dedicated characters whose actions entwine over distances and beyond their own comprehension. Like any world worth living in, the Lands have humor, mystery, horror and action to delight and entertain the reader.

available as eBook and in print
ISBN 978-3-95681-066-4